**Revenge - Text copyright © Emmy Ellis rev 2020
Cover Art by Emmy Ellis @ studioenp.com © 2020**

**All Rights Reserved**

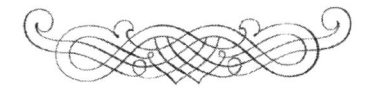

*Revenge* is a work of fiction. All characters, places, and events are from the author's imagination. Any resemblance to persons, living or dead, events or places is purely coincidental.

The author respectfully recognises the use of any and all trademarks.

With the exception of quotes used in reviews, this book may not be reproduced or used in whole or in part by any means existing without written permission from the author.

Warning: The unauthorised reproduction or distribution of this copyrighted work is illegal. No part of this book may be scanned, uploaded, or distributed via the Internet or any other means, electronic or print, without the author's written permission.

# REVENGE

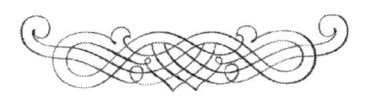

Emmy Ellis

# Chapter One

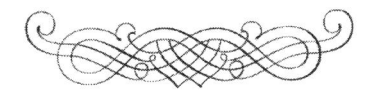

The Cardigan Estate wasn't its official name, just something the residents called it, and it wasn't just one estate but many in a section of London. Debbie's boss, Ronald Cardigan, ran the area, what with him owning all the pubs in these parts. Some said 'estate' meant him thinking he was lord of the manor.

He was, he just didn't have the official title.

She smiled in turn at everyone in The Angel, the pub she managed for him, but in reality, she'd roped someone else in to do it. How could she oversee that job plus run the brothel out the back?

Mindful Massage was a lucrative venture.

Who'd have thought a prostitute could swan around in luxury? She certainly hadn't. Years ago, as a wet-behind-the-ears novice standing on the street corner freezing her tits off, she'd been a million miles away from riches, snatching money off punters before the deed began, stuffing it in her cheap little handbag.

Now, she had a Prada and no need to go out into the darkness and ply her trade in her scuffed high heels, her bare legs cold as fuck, and her teeth chattering. It paid to be nice to Cardigan, and he'd rewarded her.

Some people were scared of him, and she'd been the same at first, but with his wife dying, he'd wanted a sample of Debbie — or Peony as she was known to the customers as soon as they stepped through the doorway to the brothel — and there was no way she could've said no.

She sipped a Coke, glancing at the massive clock on the wall to the right, one she'd had put up as a joke so customers didn't have to squint to check the time when they were rat-arsed. She'd have to go to work soon. Just fifteen minutes left until the nightly shenanigans.

Shirley Richmond walked in and stood beside her, smelling of jasmine and whatever else was in her perfume. Her black hair came from a bottle, different from her original blonde—"Brassy for a brass," she'd once said, "so I fancy going darker." Her skinny frame and big tits were the envy of many a woman. She smiled, her teeth recently whitened at the dentist, and the action raised her beauty spot above her top lip. "All right?"

Debbie nodded. Shirley didn't have a 'sex name', said her own was good enough. If men didn't like it that she didn't have something exotic, they could go and do one. She'd knocked around with a fair few fellas, had an on-off relationship with Mickey Rook once upon a time, but it fizzled out after a massive barney because she wouldn't stick her finger where it wasn't supposed to go. His mate, Harry Findley, had also sniffed around her, although Mickey had no idea his friend had sampled the goods, too.

"Ready for work then?" Debbie asked, wondering if she should add some highlights to her auburn hair next time she had a moment to nip to the salon down the road. She felt a bit mousy at the minute.

"Not really. Can't say opening my legs after all these years is still appealing, but whatever, I can't do anything else."

"You're only twenty-six." Debbie swirled her finger in the little puddle the condensation from her glass had formed on the bar. "You talk like you're all washed up."

"I feel it sometimes." Shirley took her compact mirror out of her bag to check her face, always mindful of what it looked like.

"The makeup's fine," Debbie said.

Fuck knows what Shirley had felt like when a man had slid a knife between her lips and pushed the blade back, giving her a permanent smile. Her skin had parted, blood had gushed, and she still wouldn't let on who'd done it.

Debbie reckoned she'd been warned to keep her new mouth shut.

*No surprise around here.*

"I'm just conscious of it, that's all." Shirley dropped her mirror back in her bag. "Reckoned my days of prossing were over when he did it, thought no man would want me. Damaged goods an' all that."

"I know you did, love."

"If it wasn't for you, I'd have been out on the streets in a different way, unable to pay my rent." Shirley smiled at Lisa, the manager Debbie had employed. "Just a lemonade, ta." She took her leather jacket off. "Bloody sweltering in here. Anyone would think it was July not May. The weather's off its rocker. Anyway, going back to what we were talking about. Like you always say, that's behind me now." Arse on a barstool, she sighed. "If I were a bloke, I wouldn't touch me with a barge pole."

Debbie elbowed her. She hated it when Shirley put herself down. "Pack that in. Your regulars like you for who you are, not what you look like. Besides, you're good in the sack."

"Or up against a wall."

They laughed.

"A car bonnet," Debbie said.

"On a grass verge. Cheers, Lisa." Shirley took a fiver out of her skirt pocket and handed it over. "Keep the change."

Lisa smiled her thanks and walked off to serve someone else. The bar was filling up, and Debbie recognised a few men who weren't really there for the beer. One of Shirley's regular fellas, Tommy Crocket, nodded at Debbie and tapped his watch.

"Six minutes, you," she called over.

"He's eager," Shirley muttered.

"Always is. What was it you said? Done in sixty seconds?"

"Poor bastard gets a bit excited. I tell you, I'm knackered." Shirley took a sip of her drink. "I didn't get much sleep, what with the bin men coming so early, then those brats in the street thumping up and down the road. Fucking elephants with fog horns, them lot."

Debbie felt a bit guilty. She had the luxury of a flat upstairs all to herself, plus she had no trouble sleeping. Once her head hit the pillow, she was out of it unless someone rang the bell. They kept odd hours, working from seven at night until three in the morning, and Debbie's 'evening' was from then until about eight or nine. She slept through until the afternoon. She'd got used to it, though. A small price to pay for having the things she did now. Flash flat, flash car, perfect for someone who flashed her knickers.

Shirley stiffened.

"What's up?" Debbie frowned.

"Look in the mirror behind the bar." She nodded at it.

Debbie took a peek. 'The Brothers' had walked in. George and Greg Wilkes, twins who worked for Cardigan. It was clear they were looking for someone who'd probably pissed her boss off.

She shrugged. "Don't mind them. They're nice when you get to know them."

Shirley bristled. "They wouldn't let it lie when they came round about this." She patted one half of her scar with a cerise fingernail. "On and on, they went, asking who'd done it."

"Only because they don't hold with women getting hurt."

"Yeah, well, they ought to just mind their own fucking business." Shirley checked the clock. "Anyway, time to go, and not a moment too soon."

They slipped off their stools, and Debbie waved at Iris and Lily, two blondes who'd just breezed through the double doors. They'd chosen flower names, as she'd suggested, and so long as they did their jobs and behaved themselves, she couldn't give a toss. Lavender swanned in next, a bit of an uptight sort, maybe with some home-life issues, and they called her Lav just to get a rise out of her. She always complained she wasn't a toilet and for them to shut their mouths. Her afro had been hidden beneath a red headscarf that matched her dress.

With the five of them present, Debbie led the way to the door marked PRIVATE round the corner down the corridor next to the loos, the perfect spot so any coppers in here for a pint wouldn't think twice of men coming in all desperate-looking then leaving with a broad smile. It could be attributed to them taking a leak, the relief on their bladder cheering them up.

Debbie chuckled to herself and unlocked the door. She walked along another corridor to a second door, which was kept locked. If anyone who didn't know about Mindful Massage via word of mouth wandered down here, they'd think it was an office. The plaque on the door said so.

Cardigan had some CCTV installed, and Debbie had a monitor on her reception desk so she could see who'd come through. They had to ring a bell, and she only let them in if she recognised them. If they were new to the game, they had to hold up their ID. It was appointment only, so those who *did* try to chance their arm got told to ring her. She handed them a business card and sent them on their way once they'd named someone Debbie knew so she could check they were okay.

She had to keep the girls and herself safe. Like Shirley had said, no one welcomed a slashed face if they could help it.

Debbie unlocked the door and held it open. The women filed into the waiting area with its expensive red carpet, black leather sofas, a couple of oak coffee tables, and a matching sideboard with a stereo on top, a potted palm in one corner—she kept forgetting to water the bugger—and a fake fern in the other. Men—and sometimes women—waited in comfort for their 'masseuse' to become available, and Debbie gave them a complimentary drink from one of the bottles in the sideboard. All very civilised.

Her employees went off to their respective rooms. They each had an en suite so they could have a quick shower between punters, and the massage beds had a function to higher or lower them, plus a second leather-covered mattress that pulled out from underneath for those customers who liked the illusion of a real double bed. To an outsider, the rooms looked like they were supposed to.

Debbie didn't use hers much anymore. It was reserved for Cardigan when he nipped in for a quickie. She was his, no one else's, and she liked it that way. She was fond of him, even though he was a lot older than her, and she couldn't fault him for his kindness while he was with her. Before he'd offered her the run of The Angel, he'd taken her to his big posh house, but she didn't like it there. His daughter was a right snob and always looked down her nose at her.

Haughty cow.

Debbie closed the door, and it locked automatically. Behind the desk, she switched on her computer, plugged in the phone, and turned the CCTV on.

It was time to become Peony.

# Chapter Two

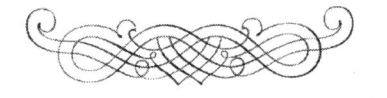

Sweat dripped down Jonathan Pembrooke's temples.

*What the bloody hell am I doing here again?*

He looked around at the other people seated at the table and tried to appear calm. Ronald Cardigan's unnerving gaze rested on him. Jonathan experienced the urge to run home to his mum, despite being over thirty years old. And he would have—if she wasn't dead.

Alone in this mess, and with nothing he could do to get out of it, he blew out through dry, pursed lips. He tried to assess the situation with a rational mind, but inside, he was anything but rational.

*I'm going to lose my fucking life let alone my mind...*

If he didn't come up with anything he could barter with, he'd be a dead man.

Ronald Cardigan would see to that.

Cardigan's near-black eyes unsettled him further. The older man ruled this patch of London, inspiring fear in anyone who crossed him.

"I've bled your coffers dry, haven't I, Pembrooke?" His wide, muscly bulk barely fitted on the carver chair, and his frame seemed to fill the small back room of the pub. Lucky for him, his games of poker for huge sums of money went undetected. He owned all the boozers in these parts.

*Greedy bald bastard.*

Jonathan's resolve to stay calm throughout the game cracked. "You've already got all my money. What the bloody hell else d'you think I can give you? My business isn't stable, and if I'm not careful, I'll go under. What d'you think I'm doing here? I haven't been playing poker with the likes of you lot for the good of my health."

Turning to his business partner, Cardigan said, "Bloody hell's bells, Sam, I think he's beginning to shit himself. Took him long enough, didn't it?"

"You're right, guv. He looks scared," Samuel Hood said, his voice thick.

All his life—even as a schoolboy—Sam had threatened and menaced people under the instruction of Ronald Cardigan. Sam idolised him and had even gone so far as killing for him.

On numerous occasions.

"Shall we let him off? Or shall we slit his throat?" Cardigan toyed with the cards.

Sam shrugged, noncommittal. "It's up to you. I'll go along with whatever you say."

*He's fucking with me. Making me sweat.*

The decision to play cards with these 'gentlemen' had been a hard one. If Jonathan's brewery business wasn't about to fold, he wouldn't be here at all.

Cardigan continued to stare at him. Long seconds passed, then, "I think I quite like you, in one way or another, Pembrooke." He paused, gazed up at the bare light bulb. Cigarette smoke curled beneath it. "I've got a proposition for you.

Look carefully at your hand of cards before you tell me if you accept."

Cardigan glared at him harder; his black irises reflected the light.

Shuddering, Jonathan stared down at his cards. "What d'you propose?"

"If you beat me, you can take all that lovely money on the table."

Jonathan eyed the bundles of notes. If he won, he could save his floundering business with plenty to spare. But there had to be a catch. There always was with Cardigan.

"And if I lose?"

"You get to marry my daughter. Isn't that nice?" Cardigan smirked at the other players, who were obviously glad it wasn't them in the hot seat. He picked a player a night to take for all he could.

Cardigan owned pubs. Jonathan owned a brewery.

If Jonathan lost, Cardigan won in more ways than one.

The other participants, all out of cash, glanced from Jonathan to Cardigan and back again. Two men had already left the table, Cardigan and Jonathan the only remaining players. The rest had stayed for the show. If Cardigan didn't get an audience, he got angry.

Taking a deep breath then letting the air out slowly, Jonathan licked his dry, cracked lips and reached for a glass of water. His throat arid, the water went down a treat. His heart hammered too fast, and the proverbial hole in the ground didn't appear to swallow him the fuck up.

Who was the daughter? He'd heard nothing about her. She must be pretty young, or else he was sure he'd know something, her being Cardigan's kid. The bastard bragged about what he had to all and sundry.

"What's she like?" Jonathan asked.

"Who, Leona?" Cardigan smiled. "A very nice girl. What else d'you expect me to say about my own flesh and blood? Dickhead..." A frown marred his forehead.

Letting fate decide, Jonathan said, "I accept your proposal." His stomach churned as he digested his words. They echoed through the room, sounded doom-filled, sealing him to a fate he wanted no part of.

"Then shake on it." Cardigan reached out his hand.

Dread grew heavy in the pit of Jonathan's stomach.

*I bet I've lost. Shit.*

Heart thrumming faster, he silently prayed.

"Your call, guv," Sam rasped in his bored monotone.

"Nah." Cardigan's grin widened. "We'll let our friend here turn over his cards first. That's how kind I am."

Jonathan glanced at his palms and shaking fingers, damp with sweat. He knew better than to argue so turned over his cards. They seemed to smirk at him from the green baize. Mocked him.

*Come on, don't let me down now. I'll do anything, just let me win the money.*

Cardigan reached out to turn his own cards over. An eerie smile played on his lips, the corners twitching. "Come to my house at eight tomorrow night. You can meet my Leona then."

---

Jonathan left The Swan and Cygnets via the back door.

What fate was worse? Death, or marriage to an unknown woman?

Dazed, he stumbled along the backstreets towards the house he'd lived in all his life. The scent of fresh rain blew past him on a rough gust of wind, and his hair danced briefly then settled back down. He stuffed his hands in his pockets and bent his head, the pavement cracked and uneven beneath his tired feet.

*Marriage...shit. There's always divorce if it doesn't work out.*

He took a deep breath then released it. Some of the tension in his head and neck bled away. Rubbing his nape, he winced at a twitching nerve.

Things would have been easier to deal with if his mother was at home waiting for him to walk in, her usual cup of tea in hand. Jonathan wouldn't have been at that card game in the first place had she been alive today. She would've seen some way to getting him out of the mess he was in with regards to his brewery. Too much credit and not enough money to pay the bills — going round on a roller coaster, unable to get off, sometimes at a high, but mainly at an all-time low, with the scary loop-the-loop in between.

Jonathan's thoughts turned to his friend, Sonny Bates.

"You'd be welcome to join in a poker game with Ronald Cardigan and try your luck at doubling or even trebling your money," he'd said.

*Or losing the fucking lot.*

Jonathan had been on edge earlier but not overly worried at the prospect of a game of cards with Cardigan. Sonny had warned him that

Cardigan picked on a certain player each night but had assured him it wouldn't be Jonathan. Sonny had got word that small-fry Mickey Rook had slighted Cardigan the previous week. Cardigan had made it clear Mickey should attend the game—if he knew what was good for him.

*Sonny wouldn't have lied to me. Cardigan must have changed his mind. Got a feeling I'm going to lose the fucking business now anyway. Cardigan'll take over. And who am I to stop him?*

Cardigan had given Mickey Rook menacing glares throughout the first half of the evening and milked him dry. At the point when Cardigan thought he'd cleared him out, Mickey produced a large wad of notes and placed the lot on the table. Cardigan had already turned over his cards.

Taking his chance to win and leave the game, Mickey whipped his cards over.

"Fix!" Cardigan had shouted. "You've fucking fixed the game, son. Did your mate here help you?" Cardigan had looked at Harry Findley. "Well? Did you?"

"No," Harry said.

Jonathan had marvelled at how calm he'd appeared. Harry was a bit dim sometimes, but even so…

Cardigan had huffed. "You'd better leave now, gentlemen, and let me tell you, you need to watch your backs in future. You needn't think I'm taking this lying down. Show them out, Sam."

"Right, guv."

Sam had heaved his massive bulk from his chair and grabbed Mickey's and Harry's arms. The door opened by one of Cardigan's goons, Sam hoisted the two men off their feet and through the opening.

In a black mood, Cardigan had turned his attention to Jonathan, who'd staked two thousand altogether throughout the entire game, pooling all his spare cash, which more than made up for what Cardigan had lost to Mickey Rook.

Jonathan sighed again. He'd been well and truly taken for a mug. Cursing himself at his stupidity in ever going to a Ronald Cardigan game in the first place, he let himself in his front door. Weary, he climbed the stairs.

Sleep evaded him. The uppermost thought in his mind? That he'd soon be meeting a woman he'd agreed to marry—without ever having set eyes on her before.

# Chapter Three

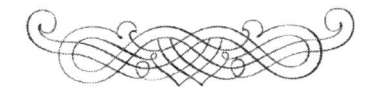

Debbie was engrossed in *Heat* magazine. She didn't jump when the door to the massage parlour opened. Cardigan had a key, the only person other than herself, and he swaggered in, his bald head gleaming beneath the light from the chandelier. He was wide and tall, muscly, fit for a sixty-something, appearing much younger, and if you bumped into him in the dark, he'd block out the moon.

"All right, Treacle?" he said, coming up to the reception desk.

He always called her that instead of her name. She liked it.

"Fine, ta. You?"

He scowled. "A bit knobbed off as it happens."

"Why's that then?" She didn't like him knobbed off. It changed his face and bearing, switching him from the man she'd come to know into the one she hadn't before he'd lowered his defences around her.

"Poker."

"Ah. Want to talk about it?"

He nodded. "All the customers in with the girls?" He glanced around the empty seating area. "Or just a slow night?"

"They're all busy. The next one isn't due for an hour."

"I timed it right then."

"You always do."

"Press the button."

She scooted across in her chair to prod the bell push that alerted the girls that she wasn't manning the desk. It meant they had to let the customers out themselves instead of her playing hostess.

Cardigan strolled over to her door, punched in a code on the pad beside the jamb, and she followed him into her room. This one had a proper bed, and if any coppers did a raid on the place, she had her excuse ready. This was where they went to rest between clients, a safe space to relax.

Cardigan shut the door. Debbie flopped on the bed and waited for him to join her. She snuggled into his side, and he cuddled her.

"Fucking Mickey Rook," he said.

Debbie sighed. "Oh dear."

"He's a pest. Cheated me. I'm going to do for that fucker."

She tried not to dwell on what Cardigan did when he wasn't with her. "Is that why The Brothers were in here earlier?"

"Yeah, I sent them scouting after Mickey had left."

"Thought so."

He squeezed her closer. "Micky wasn't in here then?"

"Nah. Haven't seen him for a while."

"Little wanker."

He went on to get everything off his chest, then mentioned Jonathan Pembrooke, someone she'd gone to school with. He was a tasty fella, not so much as a teenager, with his spots and prominent

Adam's apple, but he'd grown into the latter, and if she wasn't exclusive to Cardigan and such a 'filthy slag' as some people called her, she might have tried her luck.

"*He* played poker?" she said, shocked.

"Yep. His brewery's on the way to being fucked."

"That's no surprise to me. It's not like all the pubs round here serve his beer, is it?"

"They will soon."

"Ah."

"He lost the game and won my daughter."

Debbie forced herself not to smile or laugh. Leona was about forty-five from what she'd gathered while chatting with Cardigan. A young bloke like Jonathan with her… Christ, what a lucky bitch. Then she felt guilty. She was happy with the man on her bed, didn't need anyone else. "Does he know how much older she is than him?"

"Nah, but he'll soon find out." He rolled on top of her and stared into her eyes. "Come on then, Treacle, do what you do best. Make me forget."

# Chapter Four

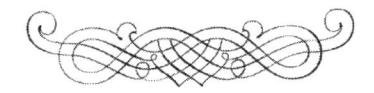

Cardigan travelled home in the back of his luxury car, Sam at the wheel.

Treacle always had a good effect on him. He got lost with her in bed, wasn't the man he'd built himself up to be for the time he was with her. Famous in the criminal underworld, he clicked his fingers to get anything sorted. His word was law; nobody crossed him on his patch—and God fucking help them if they did. A widower, he had the choice of many from a string of floozies, none of which lasted very long, and now he had Treacle, he didn't want anyone else. Nobody could match up to his late wife, Katherine, but his search for happiness in a relationship that had so far eluded him was on the up now.

He thought of Leona, still living at home. She disapproved of his lifestyle, forever trying to make him see the 'error of his ways'. He laughed quietly. Her and her adopted posh accent—she'd taken the fact they had money a little over the top, modelling herself on an old school friend she'd had years ago. Becky something or other. Silly cow. He kept telling her it was in the breeding, not the way you presented yourself. People knew when you were from class. And they most certainly weren't.

*Bloody proud of my roots, I am.*

He'd grown up piss poor, his earlier life hard. He'd joined a proper gang soon after marrying Katherine, a motley crew of youngsters, and they'd robbed a bank. His share of the money had come in handy and enabled him to purchase his first pub, The Stag.

As man and wife, they'd enjoyed the high life, and he'd built up his empire, vowing to

Katherine he'd go on the straight and narrow and run The Stag legitimately. They'd worked side by side until Leona was born. Then Katherine spent the majority of her time looking after their daughter and suggested they buy a house.

He saw her in his mind now, his beautiful wife.

"I don't want our little girl being brought up in the pub atmosphere," she'd said.

He leant his head against the car seat and brushed away a treacherous tear—Katherine was his soft spot—drifting back to the past once more.

Inevitably, the shady deals going on in his pub turned him back to crime. He'd be the leader of such matters if they occurred in his own establishment. With Katherine safely out of the way at the new house, he'd joined in on the numerous crimes she incredulously read about in the local newspaper. Using his share of the money from various schemes, he bought another pub, The Three Horseshoes. He employed a manager for each public house and devoted his time to working his way up.

Frightening people came naturally to him, as did lending money with extortionate interest rates or pimping women out on shadowy street corners. To him it seemed he earned money for doing nothing.

Cardigan's thoughts moved back to the present. Leona would be a hard obstacle to get over. She'd been getting right on his nerves lately, hence him setting her up as the prize in tonight's poker game. He'd just have to persuade her that it was in her best interests.

*I'm not having my mates feeling sorry for me. I've heard the bloody wisecracks about how ugly Leona is. I'll make her see sense.*

He glanced out of the window. "Drop me off on the corner, Sam. Take the car with you. I fancy a bit of fresh air. A good brisk walk'll do me nicely. You can take the rest of the night off, because I've got Leona to sort out."

"Right, guv."

# Chapter Five

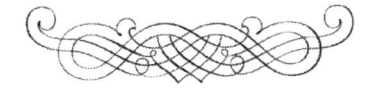

Incensed, Leona Cardigan paced the living room. She caught sight of herself in the large mirror that hung over the open fireplace. Bright-red cheeks gave her a more severe appearance. A long, pointed nose and thin pale lips didn't help either. Her lacklustre hair, brown peppered with early grey and scraped into a bun, pulled her features back.

Married? What was her father thinking?

"What?" she screeched.

He winced and took a sip of his whiskey. "Don't shout like that. I've got an almighty bloody bonce ache." He rested his head on the back of his burgundy leather wing chair.

"Why shouldn't I shout when you come in here and tell me something like that? How did it all come about? A business deal?"

"Nah, you were won in a game of poker." He roared with laughter.

"A game of poker?"

"I thought you'd be pleased. It can't be nice knowing no one wants you. Besides, you're getting on my nellies, moping around the house like a bloody dog."

That was a bit harsh, but she supposed she wasn't anything like the daughter he remembered from years ago. She'd changed into a woman he despised most of the time.

"I've got my charity work, that keeps me busy. And how can you say I mope around the house? It's all right for you, what with your ventures. You've got some sort of focus in your life."

He swigged a large gulp of whiskey. "Ah, but I know how you feel, not having that special person in your life, don't I? I always had your mother, and now I haven't."

"What about your slappers? Don't they provide what you're missing? You look like you're enjoying yourself with them, and they were in the house often enough. It disgusts me."

He waved a hand at her impatiently. "So you keep saying. They kept me young, and anyway, I don't bring them here anymore. And we've conveniently got off the subject. I thought you'd be grateful for what I've done. You always were a hard one to please once you hit your teens, with your trumped-up ideas and your stuffy way of gassing."

Leona bit back a spiteful retort and swallowed. "So, who is this man I'm supposed to be getting married to?"

"He's called Jonathan Pembrooke. Owns a brewery, so you'll not go short of cash once I start buying his beer. There will always be drinkers. He's about thirty, but—"

"Thirty? He's fifteen years younger than me. I don't believe the level you've sunk to. And how convenient he owns a brewery. It was a business deal after all. You make me sick."

He ignored her outburst, smoothing a palm over his head. "He'll be here tomorrow night about eight. Make yourself presentable. You know I don't go back on a deal, so you'll just have to like it or lump it—or fuck off out from under my roof and make your own way. I'll be putting money into his business because it needs a bit of help, and I want you to work for him. Keep an eye on it. He'll be thinking he can still run it on his own, but he's got another think coming."

"Me?" Leona's mouth hung open. "You've got a cheek, you have. I refuse to do it. I won't marry someone I don't even know, just so you can join your empires together."

"You will bloody marry him, my girl. You don't bleedin' go back on what I've said. And if you do, like I just said, move out and pay your own way for a change. Get a bloody job."

Leona stormed out and thumped upstairs to her dressing table. She sat on the stool and looked in the mirror, wanting to see herself as someone else would. Her bony nose dominated. Dull grey eyes slanted downwards. She cringed, and her face screwing up into an unattractive expression brought on tears.

*Who in their right mind would want to marry me anyway?*

Business reasons, the root of the deal. Her father must have let the man know what the poker stake was. No sane person would agree to marry someone without first knowing who they were and what they looked like, surely?

Throughout the night she stayed awake, coming to the conclusion, after the initial shock had worn off, that getting married to this Jonathan Pembrooke wouldn't be so bad. Him being younger, it'd look like she had the ability to snare any man she wanted. Everyone in her circles would think he loved her and had chosen to marry her, ugly or not.

Being married would give her a sense of belonging, and even though he'd never take the place of her beloved William, she'd try her hardest to get along with him. They'd be engaged for quite some time—she needed to become accustomed to this strange thing happening in her life, something she'd never envisaged happening at all.

With sleep still evading her, she got out of bed and padded over to her mirror again. She'd at least kept her trim figure. She supposed it may have been because she'd never had any children. Thinking of her age, she wondered if it would be possible to still try for a baby. She shuddered at what she'd have to go through to achieve that. Maybe she'd find this Jonathan attractive?

'Doing it' wouldn't seem so bad then.

# Chapter Six

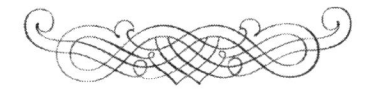

Rebecca Lynchwood sighed. Her loneliness at becoming a widow after her husband died ten years ago scratched at her mind. She thought of him now, conjured up his image in an attempt to convince herself he was still there. Still with her. William had been the be all and end all for her, apart from their daughter, Gracie. His death of heart failure at thirty-six had transformed her life from one of happiness to one of total despair.

Tears stung her eyes, and a lump formed in her throat.

She remembered how she'd fallen in love with him, how she'd come close to losing him—or so she'd thought back then—after their engagement. Someone else had their eye on him without her knowledge, had schemed to steal him away from her. This woman really thought she'd succeed, too, and she might have if Rebecca hadn't listened to William.

She imagined being that younger version of herself now, looking at the scene as if on the outside, as though she was that fresh-faced girl with the rest of her life ahead of her. If only she knew then what she knew now. She might have loved William a little more, hugged and pleased him a little more, worried a little less.

She'd left school and started work at Plumbstead's solicitors where she'd met Leona Cardigan. Rebecca didn't need to work, her family were well-to-do, and her parents frowned on the friendship she'd formed with someone they called 'that common girl'. That common girl, however, had just as much money in her family as they did in theirs.

She recalled what her mother had once said: "They're the sort who think they're somebody just because they've built themselves up from the slums."

Despite her parents' opinions, she continued her friendship with Leona, who proved to be a good laugh.

Until Rebecca met William.

She saw him—one of those common people, too—as many nights as she could. Leona claimed to know him well from her school days and, as Rebecca had an idea Leona felt left out, she'd asked her if she'd like to join them on their dates. Leona had agreed—a bit too eagerly.

*I should have sensed something then.* She sighed again. *God, that girl knew exactly what she was doing.*

Tears pooled and fell, and she wished she could turn back the clock, wished she could tell him everything she hadn't instead of saying it to a ghost.

*"Leona seems to think she knew you well at school," Rebecca said one night while they strolled back from dropping Leona off.*

*William let out a mirthless laugh. "I didn't know her very well. All the boys used to take the piss out of her. She thought she was something special because her old man had money. I got the shock of my life when I saw her again. You know, when you wanted your friend to join us. Once I realised it was her, I nearly pissed myself."*

*"She seems to think you were really good friends."*

*"In her bloody dreams maybe."*

*Rebecca's frisson of jealousy died down. William was hers and hers alone.*

*One night, shortly after Rebecca and William's secret engagement, she came down with a nasty bout of flu. William, feeling sorry for Leona, all dressed up and nowhere to go, asked Rebecca if she'd mind him taking Leona out anyway.*

*"You just keep your hands to yourself," she joked.*

*"Give me some bloody credit."*

*Rebecca went to bed and snuggled up, safe in the knowledge that William would behave.*

*Her mother came in and sniped, "Just one night away from them is better than none. Here, drink this cocoa and eat some toast."*

*Amazingly, the next day, Rebecca felt one hundred percent better and went to work, ready to bombard Leona with questions as to how their evening had gone. Rebecca's enquiries fell on deaf ears. Leona wasn't at work. Guessing she'd caught her bug, she shrugged it off, intending to telephone her friend as soon as she got home to find out all the gossip.*

*She walked down her street after work, anxious to phone Leona. She turned to enter her driveway, and*

*William jumped out of the tall hedges that lined the path and grabbed her.*

*Rebecca squealed and smacked a palm against her chest. "William! What are you playing at?" Her cheeks warmed from fright, and her heartbeat went wild.*

*William clasped her elbow and pulled her along the street. They reached the corner, and he looked from left to right then turned her to face him. "I didn't mean it. She made me do it. It wasn't my fault."*

*"What? What are you talking about?"*

*"She's a bloody nutter. Gives me the creeps. Talk about make the hairs on the back of my neck stand up." William's eyes narrowed as if he'd brought an image back to mind.*

*"Calm down and start again."*

*"Didn't she tell you? She said she would. Said me and her could be together. She's a fucking crackpot."*

*"Tell me? Tell me what? She wasn't at work today. Look, go through the evening."*

*"Right. I took Leona out, like you said I could. To the pictures. I really wanted to watch that film an' all, but she kept chatting. She got the message that I wasn't listening after a while and shut up. Just when it got to the really juicy bit, she turned round in her seat and told me how much she loved me, said she had done for years, ever since we were at school."*

*Rebecca's heart skipped a beat. "Is that all she did?"*

*"No, I'm afraid not."*

*Rebecca fought to come to terms with the fact that she might hear something she'd rather not, but determination to hear William out won the battle raging inside her. She looked at him, acknowledged the state he was in, and waited for him to speak.*

*"After she'd gone on about loving me for God knows how long, she gripped the back of my neck and kissed me." William swallowed. "I didn't respond, I swear. I just wanted to get her mouth away from mine, so I shoved her. She cried out, from the shock I reckon. I wouldn't do anything to hurt you, but there's something else I have to tell you. Don't go mad at me now…" He inhaled deeply, blowing out through shaky lips. "When she was getting out of her seat, she said she was going to tell you that I'd kissed her and then she could have me all to herself. I don't ever want to see her again."*

*William's sincerity was so obvious that Rebecca found it difficult not to believe him.*

*"I don't want to see her again either." She called his bluff, just in case. "But I want a few words with her first."*

*Leona denied the whole episode at the cinema at first. "I don't know what you're going on about, Rebecca." She sounded offended. Her accent had changed since she'd been friends with Rebecca; her harsh London brogue had disappeared, and a softer, mellow tone had taken its place with nicely rounded vowels, although sometimes, when angry or excited, her true accent came out.*

*"You don't know what I'm going on about? So, I suppose William's lying then? Is that what you're saying?"*

*"That's right. He's is lying. He wants you all to himself and resents me because he has to share you."*

*"Resents you? He's welcomed you on all of our dates, taken us both. You're really ungrateful."*

*"Don't use that tone with me. Who do you think you are?" Leona snapped.*

*"A damn sight better than you, I know that much." Rebecca smiled. "If what you're saying is true and William is lying, you won't mind telling him that to his face in front of me, will you?"*

*Leona's face reddened, and she blustered, "I don't need to say anything of the sort to his face. I don't have to prove anything."*

*"It's you who's the liar."*

*Leona's cheeks turned a deeper shade of red. "All right, you've asked for it. I did tell him that I wanted him, an' I did kiss him. Now what are you goin' to do about it, you silly cow?"*

*"I'm going to do nothing at all. Because he loves me." Rebecca moved to walk away but couldn't resist a parting shot. "Oh, and one other thing. My mother was right after all. You* are *common."*

Satisfaction raged through Rebecca with the memory of that altercation. Nowadays, because of Leona, she didn't let herself get close to anyone. Her daughter was the only one she relaxed her guard with. She'd never be taken for granted by a friend again.

Oh, those days were gone now. She missed having William to turn to for support. His premature death had spun her into oblivion for months, and she'd been unable to come to terms with the fact she'd hardly begun her life with him, that she'd never see him walk through that front door again.

Tears spilled down her cheeks. She'd never get over the death of her husband and would do anything to have him back. She'd also do anything in her power to get back at Leona Cardigan, who she'd heard was a spindly old hag with no one to love her. Pleasure had soared through Rebecca's system when she'd heard that information. She sneered, knowing she'd never find it in her heart to forgive Leona.

*One day, I'll make her pay.*

# Chapter Seven

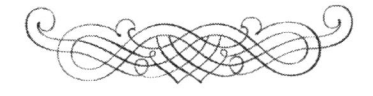

Sitting on the bus on her way to work, Gracie pondered on the direction her life was going. She loved every aspect of her world at the moment, except for not having a bloke. All she needed was someone to love her. Finding him was another matter, but it wasn't for the want of trying.

She'd convinced herself she'd been looking in all the wrong places and, at twenty-two, realised it was time to climb down from the shelf and take the business of finding a boyfriend seriously.

Mum had asked her to go to the theatre with her. The chances of meeting anyone there were slim, but it couldn't hurt to try.

She stepped off the bus directly outside Plumbstead's—the same place as Mum had worked—and entered the building.

There was no more time to think about the lack of a man in her life.

# Chapter Eight

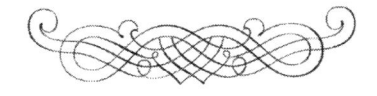

Debbie woke earlier than usual and stretched, reaching behind her to open the curtains. Afternoon sunlight streamed in. She had to get her arse out of bed. Shirley was coming round for breakfast. They'd planned it in the early hours just as the girls were leaving, Shirley saying she was down in the dumps. A new customer had called her ugly once he'd clapped eyes on her face.

Debbie wouldn't be letting him back again. The cheeky bastard looked like the back of a bus, and he was fat round the middle an' all, so what room did he have to bloody talk? Poor Shirley had cried, saying she'd be jacking it in if one more man said anything like that.

Out of bed, Debbie walked into her en suite and had a quick shower. She still smelt of Cardigan's aftershave that had rubbed off on her skin.

He'd told her about his dead wife, saying she was the love of his life and that Debbie reminded him of her. She ought to be creeped out by it, but she wasn't. Too many men to count had asked her to pretend to be their wives, women who no longer had the energy to shag them, and she'd done it to make money.

Cardigan also told her he didn't express himself to just anyone. "You're special to me, Treacle," he'd said, "and I know you won't open your gob."

No, she wouldn't. He'd kill her if she did, and besides, she liked being his floozy and could admit she'd got a tad jealous that he'd taken other women to his house. One-night stands, he'd called them, people who took the edge off when

Debbie was busy. Truth be told, she'd press the button behind the desk anytime he walked into the parlour, was never too busy for him.

She stepped out of the shower, telling herself off for getting attached.

"Stupid cow. Like he's going to make you permanent. He'll never marry anyone else, he said so."

She took some leggings and a baggy T-shirt out of the wardrobe, sending a text letting him know not to nip up to her flat, she had Shirley coming. He replied, sending her three kisses, and she got all silly, wishing they meant more than they did.

The doorbell rang, so she went to the intercom and lifted the phone. "Yep?"

"It's me."

"Come up." Debbie pressed the button to unlatch the door at the side of the pub and imagined, with every clang of footsteps, Shirley climbing the steel steps that led up here. She opened the door and smiled. "How are you feeling today? Shut the door after you."

Shirley gave the thumbs-up, looking trendy in her pink Adidas tracksuit. She'd probably been to the gym, hair in a high ponytail, damp from a shower after.

"I take it that means you're fine." Debbie wandered into the kitchen with all its mod cons, the room done out with pure-white walls, her appliances black. They were a sod to keep smudge-free, so it was a good job it was only her she had to clean up after, wasn't it.

Frying pan out of the cupboard, she stood in front of the hob. Shirley came in and plopped onto a stool at the breakfast bar. She dumped her bag on the black granite top with white veins running through it and took off her fitted trackie jacket.

"I decided, once again, to fuck what men think of me." She stuck her elbows on the surface and propped her chin in her hands. "Bloody bastard. Where did he get off saying that?"

"It's exactly what he must have done." Debbie took eggs, bacon, and sausages out of the fridge.

"What are you on about?"

"He got off on being a wanker. You know how some of them are. It probably gave his maggot a bigger thrill." She busied herself putting the sausages on a tray for the oven.

"Yeah, he's about four inches hard if I'm any judge."

They wet themselves at that, and Debbie had a moment of being so glad she'd met Shirley all those years ago out on the street. They'd stood together, watched out for each other, and if she had a best friend, she'd say Shirley was it.

They chatted for a bit while the sausages cooked, then Debbie fried the eggs and bacon and shoved beans in the microwave. She dished up, and they ate side by side, Shirley saying a good fry-up after the gym kind of negated her efforts, but what the hell.

Stomach full, Debbie made coffee and padded into the living room. She'd clean up later, stuff it all in the dishwasher and leave it to do its magic. Shirley joined her on the sofa, and they spent a good couple of hours putting the world to rights, mainly by discussing the clients and their weird quirks.

"Tommy's the worst," Shirley said.

"I'm not sure I want to know."

"You do."

Debbie smiled. "Go on then."

"He likes me pinching his toes and wiggling them." Shirley leant back after delivering that and pulled a 'fucking weirdo!' face.

"What?" Debbie shuddered. She didn't do toes.

"Yep, says his wife won't go near them."

"I don't bloody blame her. Why does he want you to do that?"

"Says it reminds him of being a kid and his mum playing This Little Piggy. When I get to the bit where the piggy runs all the way home, he grabs me and shoves it in."

Debbie held her hand up. "Nope, no more."

Shirley roared with laughter. "The things we do to pay the rent, eh, messing about with people like Tommy Toes."

---

Debbie sat behind the reception desk. Tonight, she had *Hello* magazine and a packet of chocolate Hobnobs to dip in her tea. All the girls were busy, so she had a few minutes to herself where she didn't have to let anyone in and pander to them, offering drinks or letting them out with a fake smile. She had the room rents to add into her Excel spreadsheet as well.

Everyone had paid up at the start of the night. She never had any trouble collecting. Might be because Cardigan would sort them if they were late in paying, plus Debbie would turf them back out onto the street corners. When you landed a job in a parlour, you bloody well counted your lucky stars.

The buzzer for the door sounded, startling her. Maybe a client had turned up early. She glanced at the CCTV monitor.

Fuck, it was that nasty bloke who'd been cruel to Shirley.

She got up and walked around the desk, leant over to grab the key, putting it in her pocket, and the pepper spray Cardigan insisted they all use if punters got lairy. Shirley hadn't when that wanker had said what he had to her, because he'd whispered it in her ear and hadn't been aggressive at all. Debbie reckoned that was scarier than physically abusing her while shouting in her face. A quiet voice sometimes brought more fear.

She opened the door, stepped out so it closed behind her, and held the spray in sight, taking the lid off. "What do you want?"

Vinny, his name was, all flabby body and a thick neck, his head shaved at a number three, a scar beside his eye where he'd sliced off a tattoo of a teardrop, one a gang member had put there in prison. He'd bragged how it hadn't hurt, using that knife on his face, but Debbie reckoned it was bullshit.

"I'm here for Shirley," he said, staring down at her.

She wondered if she was supposed to be scared. She would have been if she wasn't under Cardigan's protection. "You're not welcome here anymore."

He eyed the pepper spray as if contemplating whether she'd really use it.

"Oh," she said, "you'll get this right in your fucking face if you give me any gyp."

He looked into her eyes. "Get Shirley."

"No. You're banned."

He moved closer, as though pepper spray in his eyes was the least of his concerns. She couldn't move back, what with the door behind her, and despite being unafraid a minute or so ago, she cursed her heart for beating too fast now.

"Step the hell away," she warned, "or Cardigan will hear about this."

He took a pace backwards.

"Another one." She glared until he obeyed. "Now, let me explain this so it's crystal clear, right? You're not seeing Shirley here anymore. You were a bastard to her, saying what you did about her face, so that's it, barred."

He ran a hand over his cheek then dropped his arm to his side. "Look, I just wanted to say sorry, all right? That's what you do, yeah? If you say sorry, you get back on their good side again."

What kind of sick bloke *was* he? "You're a tosser. Only abusers do that."

He shook his head. "I'm not one of those."

"Yeah, you are. Now piss off." She held the spray up, ready to blast him with it.

He took a step forward. "I'm telling you, woman—"

"And I'm telling you." She pointed at the camera with her free hand. "That goes not only to my monitor but Cardigan's laptop and phone."

"Fuck."

"Yeah, fuck. Go on, sod off. If I see you here again, I'll get him to send someone to pay you a visit."

Vinny laughed. "He doesn't even know where I live."

"Nope, but I do." She reeled off his address. "I make it my business to find out before anyone's allowed past this door, so if you know what's good for you…"

He turned and walked up the corridor. At the other door, he glanced over his shoulder. "You really should have just let me say sorry."

Vinny walked out, and Debbie stared while the door slowly closed.

*Tosser.*

# Chapter Nine

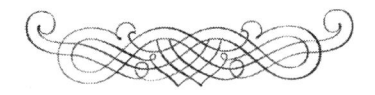

Jonathan finished knotting his navy-blue tie and put on his matching suit jacket. He hadn't finished getting his stomach in knots, though, and he reckoned he'd be busy doing that until he finally came face to face with Leona Cardigan. No matter how hard he'd tried to wheedle information out about her from people in the know, all he got in reply was "Find out for yourself" followed by ribald laughter. News had obviously spread fast, and Jonathan, getting into his car to make his way to the Cardigan household, supposed he'd have to wait and see.

Driving through the rain, he left the place where he grew up and drove to the posh part of the estate.

*He must have made a sodding packet to live where he does.*

He turned the corner into Vandelies Road and cruised past the houses until he copped sight of the number twelve on the post of a gate. He swerved into the drive and parked in front of one of the two garage doors. Took a sharp intake of breath. Cardigan's place had carefully tended gardens at the front. The house, built with grey stone and bigger than the others, hogged the land it sat on. Huge bay windows on the ground floor flanked heavily studded double front doors. A welcoming light flooded from the windows into the darkness outside, illuminating the flowerbeds beneath them. Bushes danced in the slight wind, nodding their leafy heads each time a splatter of rain touched them.

Jonathan peered through the windscreen into a bay window. From what he could tell, the decor inside looked posh—as if he could expect anything less. Cardigan always bragged about what he had and how much it cost. Jonathan had heard a lot about him and knew that by marrying into his family he'd at least be safe. He'd have Cardigan's protection to fall back on should he ever tread on anyone's toes.

He stepped out of the car, limbs shaking, and paused to steady his nerves. Not only was he going to meet his future wife, but he'd be in Cardigan's house. No one outside the man's circle would want to come here unless they absolutely had to.

Walking towards the doors, he tried to tell himself he could get out of this if he really wanted to, yet knowing in his heart Cardigan would have him taken out if he refused to marry his daughter.

Jonathan pressed the bell button and wasn't surprised at a tinkling of sound emanating through the doors, out into the night air. A nervous laugh escaped him. Cardigan wouldn't be satisfied with the normal run-of-the-mill two-tone bell.

One of the doors opened.

Cardigan's bulk filled the space. "You came after all. Good man. Bang on time, too. I'm impressed. Come in, through to the sitting room we keep for visitors. Drink?"

Jonathan followed him into the room via a large reception hallway. He glanced at the expensive furniture. Oriental rugs strategically placed on the floor gave a rich feel. A fire raged in the grate, surrounded by a huge oak mantelpiece. He couldn't fault Cardigan's taste.

He cleared his throat. "I'll have a whiskey, thanks."

"Sit down," Cardigan boomed. "I'll go and call Leona once I've made your drink."

Jonathan sat on a studded leather sofa with his back to the door. Cardigan poured the whiskey and turned to face him, his gaze flicking to the doorway.

"Oh, here she is now. Jonathan, meet my Leona."

Jonathan stood. His nerves jangled. He spun round to face her.

*She's well old. She must be his fancy bit.*

His guts twisted while Leona openly appraised him. She gave him the once-over and smiled as if pleased with what she saw.

*She may very well look at me like I'm something she's buying, but if it is her I've got to marry, that's all she will be doing, looking.*

He cleared his throat again. "Nice to meet you, Leona."

An expression of horror passed over her face. Her grimace quickly passed, leaving a stony glare in its place. Wrinkles deepened beside her eyes and mouth. "I'm very well, thank you. It was kind of you to ask."

*Sarky cow.*

Her makeup had been piled on thickly. And her accent. Where the hell did that come from? Cardigan's crackly tones were a sharp contrast to his daughter's. At the thought that this woman could belong to Ronald Cardigan, Jonathan hid a snort of laughter under a theatrical cough.

Cardigan grinned. "Come here and have a seat, Leona. Next to Jonathan there."

She walked round the sofa and perched herself on the edge, clasping her hands in her lap. His leg accidentally brushed her thigh, and she jumped two inches. She glanced at him sharply, and Jonathan let out wry laughter.

Cardigan turned from the drinks cabinet, his features twisted. "What's so bloody funny, Pembrooke?"

"Come on now, Cardigan. The joke's over. You've kept it up for long enough."

Cardigan stepped forward, his countenance menacing. "Joke? What bloody joke? I haven't done anything funny. And you're beginning to annoy me. What's there to laugh about?"

Heat rose on Jonathan's face.

*Shit.*

Cardigan's shoulders straightened, and he puffed out his chest. His face reddened. Leona stared at Jonathan. Her nostrils flared, and her lips curved downwards.

The feeling in Jonathan's gut had turned swiftly from unease to jarring splinters. "Nothing's funny. I think it's just my nerves playing me up. Sorry."

He shifted uncomfortably, away from Leona, and crossed his legs so he didn't touch her again. He sorted through his racing mind—he had to accept Leona as his lot or be bumped off. His heart throbbed hard, and he reached forward to get his drink from the glass-topped coffee table.

Cardigan relaxed his shoulders. "Now that you've controlled yourself and apologised, I'll leave you both to it. Get acquainted." He rested his gaze on Jonathan for scant seconds then stomped out, slamming the door.

Leona stood and walked across to sit opposite on a matching sofa. She seemed relieved to have some space between them. "You're not what I expected."

Jonathan swallowed. "You're not what I had in mind either. And that's putting it mildly."

Her mouth formed an 'O' of surprise, and her eyebrows lifted. "And just what do you mean by that?"

"Well, not being rude, but you're older than me. I thought you'd be younger, to tell the truth."

Purple blotches appeared on her cheekbones. Her eyes widened. She stood, her face twitching. Her cheeks puffed in and out, and she marched to the door on stiff legs. He turned towards her and watched her fight to regain composure.

"I'll say good evening," she said, her hand poised over the door handle. "We'll have a more civilised conversation next time."

Once the door slammed behind her and she stomped up the stairs, the door opened again.

Cardigan walked in. "That was a short meeting. Now then." He ran the fingers of his left hand up and down a blue file he held in his other hand. "We've just got some formalities to attend to before we discuss anything to do with the wedding."

Jonathan's stomach muscles bunched. "Formalities? What d'you mean?"

Cardigan strolled over to the sideboard and placed the file down. He picked up a full whiskey bottle, took it to the sofa Leona had vacated, and set the booze on the table between them. After pouring two large measures into both of their glasses, he handed one to Jonathan.

*Does he want to get me half-cut?*

The first whiskey already raged through his blood, and he resolved to sip the next one. He wanted to stay alert. Plus, he'd driven here.

Cardigan made himself comfortable. The sofa hissed and creaked its protest at his bulk. "Your brewery. What state is it in?"

*Business-like and straight to the point. What's he playing at?*

"There are a few debts hanging over my head." Jonathan sipped his drink and swallowed. He winced at the burn.

"Well, I'll put the money in to make the business viable again."

An order, not a request.

Although Cardigan wasn't a man to fuck with, Jonathan was proud of the business he'd built up from nothing more than a dilapidated brewery that had been long out of business and sold to him by an old man. His protective streak came to the fore, and he strove to keep his composure.

"I don't want any of your money, thanks all the same. The lull in business will soon pick up, and then I'll be able to pay all my bills."

Cardigan glared at him with widened eyes. "No. I don't think you quite understand. I want my Leona to be married and know she can live in the style she's become accustomed to. Call it a wedding present, if you like. Whatever, but I'm going to give you some money to clear all the debts."

Jonathan sighed inwardly and took a moment to think about what he was going to say. "Not wanting to get your back up, but I don't want your money. Now, if you let me sell you my beer so you can use it in your pubs, well, that'd be different altogether."

Cardigan's face lit up. "You'd need my business to get your brewery back on track?"

"You could put it like that, yeah."

The smile on Cardigan's face unnerved Jonathan.

"That'll be fine then. I'll start ordering beer from you as of tomorrow. I'll continue to buy it for as long as you keep my kid happy. I'll let her know all about it. Get my meaning?"

Jonathan got it well enough. He could keep his business going, providing he stayed married to Leona and Cardigan bought the beer. Rubbing his forehead and calculating that he'd have to get some more people to buy his stock as well, he told himself he'd be married to Leona for as long as it took to get himself back on an even keel. With the extra customers he was determined to find, he'd keep afloat after he'd divorced her.

He stared at the reflection of the chandelier on the glass-topped coffee table.

"Sign here then." Cardigan poked at a dotted line with a pen.

Jonathan picked up the papers and read them through. No hidden clauses, so he signed with a shaking hand.

Cardigan snatched the papers up. "Good, good." He heaved himself standing and walked to the drinks cabinet, opening a drawer and placing the file inside.

Jonathan's mind worked quickly.

*If my business can be saved by Cardigan's money, there'd be no need to marry. I'll make out we didn't get on, force Leona to end our relationship, and I'll be off the hook.*

"I thought a summer wedding next year would be all right," he said.

Cardigan turned to face him. "Think I'm stupid, do you? You're getting married in two weeks' time, mate. Summer wedding, my arse." He huffed out a breath and returned to his seat.

The sofa almost yelped in pain.

"Oh, right." *Shit!* "Hang on, that can't be right. You have to give notice to marry."

"Yeah, right," Cardigan said. "Not me. I know someone who'll push it through or get his head caved in. It'll be registry office, because then it can be done quick. I suggest you come and visit Leona every night to make it all look plausible. You can get to know her at the same time."

*Play along.*

"Same time each night?" Jonathan asked.

"Yeah, that'll do. Well, that's our business attended to. See you tomorrow."

Cardigan rose and stood with his arm extended, ready to shake hands. For the second time in twenty-four hours, Jonathan had to agree on a deal with Cardigan, and he felt just as sick as he had the first time.

"See you at eight," he managed.

Despondency made itself at home inside him.

*What a fucking mess. How the hell am I going to get out of this? It's literally marry Leona or die.*

# Chapter Ten

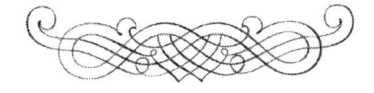

Jonathan drove home. He walked to his local, The Eagle, which Cardigan just happened to own. Situated at the end of Jonathan's street, spanning the corner, the pub was one of the smaller ones, managed by Jack Pleasant and his wife, Fiona. Any trouble there was soon sorted out. Jack's reputation for having a dangerous right hook preceded him.

Jonathan walked in, glad to be on home turf.

Jack bellowed, "All right, my old son? I hear wedding bells are in the air. You're a dark horse, getting married to none other than my boss' daughter."

Derisive laughter sailed out from various customers.

Jonathan wanted to give them all a beating. He clenched his fists and held them down by his sides. "Have a good laugh, why don't you. I don't find it bloody funny. Shall I tell my future father-in-law that you're taking the piss?"

Jack's face took on a downtrodden look.

"Give me a pint of beer. I need it tonight."

Jack stood. "I should think you do. I'm glad I'm not in your shoes. That Leona's got a tongue that could make you bleed should you get on the sharp side of it."

Jonathan sat on a stool. "You should be seeing a fair bit of blood and gore then, because I've already become acquainted with her tongue."

The crowd jeered and whistled.

Jack slapped his palm on the bar. "Well, bugger me. Did you hear that, fellas? He's already been acquainted with her tongue—and he only met her tonight. Bleedin' hell, Johnny, she must have really taken a shine to you."

*Dirty-minded bastards.*

The other men's laughter changed places with normal chatter, and the door opened. A breeze bustled in along with Sonny Bates, soaked from the rain.

"There you are. Where've you been? I've been trying to find you since last night. You're not usually so hard to get hold of." Sonny's black hair hung down against his face, wet and dripping. Not waiting for Jonathan to answer, he turned to Jack. "Throw us a towel, mate. My hair's sopping."

A clean bar towel landed on his head. The usual crowd laughed again, and Sonny stuck his middle finger up and sat on a stool next to Jonathan.

"Heard the news, have you?" Jonathan asked.

Sonny dried his hair. "I have. What the hell are you going to do? Got any way to get out of it?"

"Of course I bloody well haven't. This is Cardigan we're talking about here, not some two-bit ponce who just thinks he's hard."

"Yeah, I know what you mean. Tough shit basically, isn't it?"

"You could say that."

"Another pint?" Sonny suggested.

"Yeah, I may as well drown my sorrows. There isn't much else I can bloody do, is there?"

"You could do a runner." Keeping his voice low, Sonny continued, "You could hop it to another country and come back when it's all died down."

Jonathan looked at his reflection in the brass beer pump opposite, his features haggard. "Or when Cardigan carks it. Get real, Sonny. You always were a dopey git. He'd come and find me if I legged it, and that Sam would still keep his ear to the ground, even if I was lucky enough to see Cardigan dead. Nah, I'm stuck with my lot and can't do a damn thing about it."

Sonny shook his head and turned to Jack, who polished glasses a few feet away. "Two more pints, please."

Jack strolled over. "Heavy session tonight, lads?"

"Probably." Sonny leant his elbows on the bar until Jack brought their fresh pints over, brimming with froth on the top. He waited for him to go to the bottom end to serve one of his cronies. "What's she like, this Leona? Tasty bit of stuff or what?"

Jonathan laughed. "You're taking the piss, aren't you? She's anything but tasty. Haven't you heard about her? Everyone else seems to think it's highly hilarious I'm marrying Cardigan's daughter. And I've got to marry her, that's all there is to it."

"I haven't heard anything. What's all the fuss about?" Sonny sipped his lager.

"Well, put it this way, she looks old enough to be my mother."

Sonny's eyes widened. "Nah, you're pulling my leg."

Jonathan took a gulp of beer. "I wish I bloody was."

They sipped their pints.

Sonny, unable to keep quiet for long, piped up again. "Some older women are quite nice-looking. Shame she isn't one of them, eh?"

Jonathan clenched his jaw. "Shut up." He sighed into his pint, and some of the remaining froth splashed up onto his face. "That's it, I'm going home." He slipped from the stool and straightened his jacket.

"Don't be so bleedin' maudlin."

"You'd be bloody maudlin if you had to marry some old bag."

"Yeah, I'd have to agree with you there. Cardigan and his mob aren't to be reckoned with. Still, you could always take a mistress, because if this Leona's as bad as you say she is, you'll not be wanting to do anything with her, will you?"

Jonathan swallowed down bile. "Don't. I'm off. Cardigan's ordering a load of barrels tomorrow, so I need to be up bright and early without a headache."

"I'll be seeing you then." Sonny raised his hand in farewell and sipped his pint, then, "Oi. Can I finish your beer?"

"Yeah."

Dejected and beaten, Jonathan left The Eagle, shoulders slumped.

# Chapter Eleven

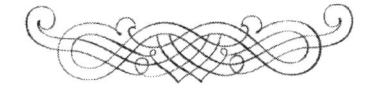

Leona had stormed up to her room in a frenzy. Mind still in a muddle, she sat on her bed. Sorting through the humiliating experience of meeting the man she was going to marry had her annoyed again.

She'd hidden her feelings and sat beside him as if unaffected. He'd deliberately touched her thigh with his leg, she knew that. Mortified at such close contact, she had to admit she'd been a little scared. She hadn't been so close to a man since that night with William in the cinema.

*I'm not what he expected.*

It should be William she was marrying. She'd kept the newspaper clipping regarding his death and frequently looked at it, envisaging her name in place of Rebecca's.

*His heart gave out because he missed me.*

But she had a new section of her life to deal with now. She'd be married to Jonathan in name only, get all the advantages of being a Mrs Somebody without all the palaver that went with it. And if Jonathan thought he could go off and get himself a mistress, he'd have to think again. She'd demand faithfulness and resolved to make his position clear at their next meeting, before any wires became crossed.

She rose and stretched her stiff muscles, then seated herself in front of her mirror and took off her makeup. She smoothed lotion over her features, dreaming William caressed her face, massaged her eyelids, and stroked her cheeks.

"I'm going to be getting married," she whispered to his ghost. "No disrespect to you."

Her father's footsteps marched past her room. *On his way to bed.*

She wiped the excess lotion from her skin and got undressed, thinking William wouldn't mind that she was marrying someone else.

He'd understand.

# Chapter Twelve

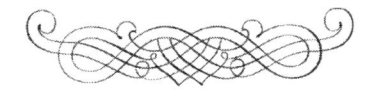

Shirley was a bit freaked out by Vinny turning up again. Debbie had told her as soon as Shirley's current client had left, and that meant she'd spent the rest of the shift worrying about it. She hadn't paid proper attention to her customers, and one of them had commented on it. She'd told him to shut up, saying she'd take twenty quid off his payment if it bothered him so much. Considering he'd once said any hole would do and he did all the work, she didn't know what he was guffing on about.

She stepped outside The Angel with Lily, Lavender, and Iris. Those three were off down the road to stand near the nightclub, The Roxy, where people milled about outside, reluctant to go home. The girls would catch some extra cash if they were lucky. Shirley didn't understand why they still touted for business when the parlour pay was more than she'd ever dreamt she'd earn. Maybe they enjoyed going back to their roots.

She shrugged and walked in the opposite direction towards home. She had a flat round the corner and halfway down the road, not as swanky as Debbie's, but she didn't have Cardigan paying her over the odds, did she, so it wasn't surprising. Still, since working at the parlour, she'd managed to update all her furniture, replacing it with stuff from IKEA, easy for her to put together by herself. No way she'd ask a man to help her.

Her heels clacked on the pavement along with the drunken shouts from folks outside The Roxy, the latter fading the farther away she got. At last, she turned the corner and let out a sigh of relief.

It seemed that corner was a portal between her two worlds, and once she rounded it, she was plain old Shirley, not the woman who spread her legs and opened her mouth for men who either couldn't get it at home, no one fancied them, or they just liked using prostitutes.

It was another warm May night, hotter than any she could remember before now, although it had been raining on and off. The air was muggy, maybe a storm on the way, and if it came before she went to bed, she'd sit at the window and listen to the thunder, watching the rain smack onto the glass and the lightning stagger across the sky, just one more drunk element of her life.

She'd grown used to men breathing on her with their beer or whiskey breath, stale cigarette smoke seeping off them the sweatier they got. She'd learnt to tune them out, pretend it wasn't happening, thinking of England sometimes but mainly about what she'd do once she'd saved lots of money. Perhaps a holiday. She could drag Debbie along, and they'd have a wicked time in Ibiza.

She approached the cemetery on the left that intersected the last house on this side of it and the one after. Sometimes, on a slow night, she looked out of her parlour room and stared at all the gravestones if the moon was bright enough to light them up. The cemetery stretched right behind The Angel, see.

Shirley took a deep breath, ready to run past the fence with its iron poles, fleur de lis on top, and the gate that was always open because some little shit kept breaking the padlock. It wasn't pitch-dark but enough to give her the creeps, and she scuttled along, chilled, as always, by the trees either side of the path that led to the cemetery, which hunched over, the branches joining in the middle to form a tunnel.

She reached the gate.

Passed it.

Someone grabbed the back of her neck, and she opened her mouth to scream, but a hand clamped over her mouth. She had the odd thought whoever it was might feel the raised surface of her scar, then it was gone, replaced by the knowledge her chest ached from fear and she was being dragged backwards, into the tree tunnel.

Her shoes came off, and the gritty tarmac dug into her heels. She snorted through her nose — *there's not enough fucking air* — and flailed her arms around in an attempt to scratch him with her nails enough so it hurt him — it had to be a him — and he let her go.

They stopped, and he threw her onto the grass, her head banging on a tree trunk. She sprang up from her hands and knees and looked around. No one was there. Breaths ragged, terror flouncing through her system, she made to run to the gate.

A figure stepped in front of her, and she bumped into a hard chest.

She'd know that smell anywhere. Vinny used that aftershave, and she hadn't smelt it on anyone else.

"I came to see you tonight," he said.

She couldn't look at his shape without shuddering so instead stared past him. A streetlight by the gate sent its brightness through, spotlighting her abandoned shoes. If someone walked by, they might notice them, come down here and see if she needed help.

In the darkness of the tunnel, she reached into her bag and felt for her phone.

"Peony wouldn't let me in," he rumbled.

Shirley found her mobile. But she couldn't use it. If she switched it on, it'd light up, and he'd see exactly what she was up to. Might get nasty. Still, she held it anyway. For comfort.

"I just wanted to say sorry." His shadow arm reached out, and he cupped her cheek.

She was glad it wasn't wet from crying. She'd refused to cry ever since her face had been cut. No man would make her do that again. They weren't special enough to produce tears. Breath held, she took her mind to that place she went when punters slobbered all over her.

"Because if you say sorry," he went on, "then everything's all right again." He paused. "Until next time."

So he was one of *those*. She should have known.

She slowly released air through pursed lips. Scrambled for something to say. Something that would appease him. "I accept your apology." That had sounded too formal, but it was out now.

"That's a good girl." He took his hand away from her face. "So you'll tell Peony you'll see me again?"

Debbie wouldn't back down now she'd barred him, but Shirley couldn't tell him that. It was too much of a risk. He could go even weirder on her, and all she wanted to do was go home. "I'll ask her, see what she says."

"Make sure you do."

He ran off down the tunnel, away from the gate, and the thought entered her mind that if The Angel wasn't closed now, he'd perv through the window if one of the girls hadn't shut the curtains.

A tremble ripped through her, and she rushed towards her shoes, scooping them up and legging it out onto her street. She didn't stop until she got home and, safe behind her locked door, she bit back treacherous tears.

No, she would *not* fucking cry.

# Chapter Thirteen

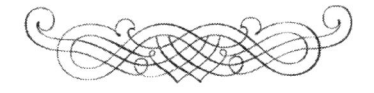

Cardigan decided to make himself scarce for the first few nights of Jonathan's visits. Let the pair of them get acquainted in peace and quiet. Everything was going according to plan, but the weather had gone to shit. A storm had raged overnight, thunder keeping him awake, as did the rain belting the crap out of his bedroom window like it had one of his scores to settle.

Sam drove him to his office. Cardigan went inside while Sam dicked about doing something in the boot.

"Get in, Sam. The bloody wind's getting in here. This weather's doing my head in. One minute you think it's going to be the start of summer, then it starts pissing it down. I tell you, it isn't doing my bones any good. I feel stiff as a board of a morning."

Sam shut the boot and ran over. He closed the office door and locked it, as was the custom. Cardigan didn't want any unwelcome visitors. An appointment had to be made before access would be given.

Sam walked over to the teak sideboard, filled the kettle, and flicked it on. Cardigan sat on a swivel chair behind his desk.

They remained in silence until Sam had sorted the tea.

"Right, down to business," Cardigan said. "I'll brief you on what's going on, and then we'll set the wheels in motion. First things first. Mickey Rook needs to be sorted. Get The Brothers to pay him a visit. He needs to know I didn't take kindly to his behaviour at the poker game. A broken leg should suffice for now. Let him know we mean business."

"Right, guv." Sam brought the cups over to Cardigan's desk. "What's next on the list?"

"Pembrooke. He's met Leona, and I got the distinct impression he was taking the piss. I'm going to let it pass this time. The second thing that needs to be sorted is the order for his beer." Cardigan took a swig of his tea, burning his tongue. "Fuck it."

He looked past Sam and out of the window. The rain beat a rhythm against the glass then turned to rivulets. Nice and cosy, he put the thought of going out into the downpour from his mind. It might stop by the time Sam took him to brief The Brothers.

"I told Pembrooke I'd order beer from him — *only* while he's with my Leona. She doesn't like it, but I told her she'll have to work for him, or at least get some kind of access to the books. My main objective is to own that brewery myself, just that Pembrooke won't know it. It might take years to get what I want, but eventually, it'll be mine." He smirked. "Once I put the squeeze on, regarding Leona not living in the style she should be, there'll be an offer made for the brewery, but not by me, if you get my meaning. Pembrooke'll have to sell up, and I'll own all the pubs *and* a brewery. What d'you think?"

"Brilliant. When do we start?"

"Right away. Cancel my order at the other gaff. Place a new one with Pembrooke. That'll keep him sweet. I'm going to be such a model father-in-law that he won't suspect a thing when it comes to him selling his business. I can see it all now. What a wanker he'll feel when he knows it's me who's bought him out."

"Yeah, a right wanker." Sam laughed and nodded.

"Get on that blower and sort out the beer. I'll just drink this tea, go for a Jimmy Riddle, and then we'll visit The Brothers. Let's hope they're not too busy to do what I want, or they'll unfortunately get up my nose an' all. Ah, anything for a quiet life."

"That's a load of bullshit, and you know it. You love the way your life is. You wouldn't change a thing, would you?"

"I'd give it all up if I could have Katherine back, you know that. But, as it isn't likely, I do what I have to."

"Then we'll make a start," Sam said, smiling.

Cardigan got wet on the way to his car, but not as much as he would have if Sam hadn't covered him with a big black umbrella. He sat on the back seat holding a handwritten, signed piece of paper for Jonathan Pembrooke.

"Nip round to Pembrooke's office first. You can get out and give him this. Saves me being drenched again."

"Yeah, like I don't mind getting wet."

"It's what you get paid for, isn't it? Doing my dirty work."

"Not dirty enough, rain. I'm looking forward to sorting Rook myself if The Brothers don't warn him right. Get myself really dirty then."

Cardigan didn't tell him he was a bit long in the tooth now for that kind of behaviour. "One thing at a time. You've got to hope Mickey ignores the warning. If he does, then you can do what you like to him. On the other hand, if the leg being broken makes him sit up and listen, I'll be that much better off, because he'll pay me back all the money he grabbed off my card table."

"He won that money fair and square."

Only Sam was permitted to point out any such thing. Being old friends from childhood had earned him that right.

"Of course he bleedin' did, but that's not the point. He was on the verge of being wiped out when he produced that wad of cash. He didn't declare he had that much money on him at the start of the game, and in my book that says he set out to con me, which he did. I don't hold with that sort of shit."

Sam looked in the rearview mirror and smiled.

"Right, park up and deliver this little note. That should give Pembrooke something to smile about."

"I'll get the umbrella then."

"No you don't. You like doing dirty work, you said it yourself, so hop it. And if you run quick enough, you shouldn't get too soaked."

Taking the note from Cardigan and racing across the yard, Sam barged into Jonathan's office and handed it over without a word. He chuckled, showing the gaps in his teeth from numerous fights years ago, and Pembrooke looked startled by it. Sam had been sneering at the thought of the rise and fall of Jonathan Pembrooke. What a laugh that'd be.

He left the office and reflected on his working life. His pay more than made up for what he did, and he'd do it for free just to be near his employer. Cardigan was good to him and always had been, seeming not to notice Sam was a little dense in the brain department. For that, Sam loved him.

He'd always do his bidding, however grotesque or mundane it was.

# Chapter Fourteen

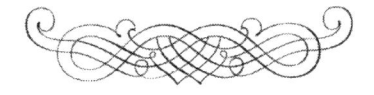

Creeped out by the eerie way Sam had smiled when handing over the much-awaited confirmation of Cardigan's order, Jonathan shivered involuntarily. A rash of goosebumps spread out over his arms, and he moved to the window to look out.

Sam sped away, Cardigan sitting in the back seat, the pair of them laughing, their heads thrown back. Jonathan shook his and opened the envelope.

Inside, a note.

He smiled. The smile turned into a wide grin. When the phone had rung earlier, with Sam on the other end requesting the beer order, Jonathan had been unsure as to whether this was one of Cardigan's jokes. The amount of barrels Sam had asked for exceeded his estimation of how much was needed. The pubs were obviously busier than he'd imagined. Had Cardigan ordered two weeks' worth?

No, this note said the same was required each week. He'd be able to get himself right out of the shit he was in quicker than he'd thought. A few more customers would have to be built up, but he was working on that. He didn't want to be left high and dry again once Cardigan wasn't ordering after the divorce.

Thinking about Leona had him remembering their conversation the night before. They'd got on better, and he'd felt more at ease once she'd announced Cardigan was out.

*She said, "Shall we start again? Neither of us are happy with this arrangement, but we could at least try and get to know one another."*

*"Excuse me for saying this, but we've both got to make the best of a bad lot, haven't we."*

*Leona turned a slight shade of crimson, and, unable to determine whether it was from embarrassment or anger, he rushed on.*

*"I don't mean to say that you're the bad lot, I meant that neither of us wants this, but I can't go back on an agreement with your old man, and you'd probably agree that'd be unwise."*

*"Yes, it would be. I wanted to make this as pleasant as I possibly could and get certain things established right from the word go." She took a deep breath. "I don't expect you to honour your conjugal rights. I certainly don't want anything to do with that side of a marriage."*

*The relief of what she'd said was immense. He had no intention of honouring his 'conjugal rights' in the slightest. Thank God she'd broached the subject. He'd planned to at some stage, though how he'd have said it was anyone's guess.*

*"That's all right then. I'm not in the habit of forcing myself on women."*

*A hopeful look swept across Leona's face. He'd said the wrong thing. Did she think he would've approached her like that?*

Jesus, no…

*"Do you mean to say you find me attractive?"*

*"It's not an issue, is it? You don't want anything of that sort, so we don't need to discuss it."*

*"No, we don't."*

*They sat in uncomfortable silence for a few minutes. Leona sipped her tea, so Jonathan followed suit and reached for his glass of whiskey. He swallowed, and the noise seemed to echo round the room. Leona winced.*

*He blurted, "Have you ever been in love? If you don't mind me asking, that is."*

*She told him about some bloke called William and how her mate stole him off her.*

*"I'm sorry to hear that. I hope to find a nice bird one day." It was strange to talk like that with someone he was marrying. If she didn't want any bedroom antics, he'd be free to look for love elsewhere, albeit discreetly. He wouldn't want to embarrass the poor woman—or piss Cardigan off.*

*"Well, that option's closed for you now. There's no way you can find someone else. We won't be married in the bedroom sense, but in all other ways I expect you to abide by the law and stay faithful to me. As you probably know, that means I won't tolerate any adulterous behaviour. The scandal would be atrocious, and I'm not prepared to be the laughingstock of my circles."*

*Jonathan found it hard to digest this piece of information. He had to get it straight in his head before he could trust himself to answer.* "So you expect me to go through my life with no one whatsoever? For as long as I'm married to you?"

"That's correct." *Leona looked bemused, as if she couldn't understand what was so daft about her suggestion.*

"Right, as long as I know where I stand."

*She cleared her throat and, changing the subject, said,* "As to the wedding arrangements, they're all finalised, bar the fitting for my dress. Everyone's had their invites sent out, so we should be receiving some replies soon."

*Jonathan's eyebrows shot up, and his mouth sagged open.* "So, you mean to tell me that everything's been done, everyone's been invited, without me being asked if I want some friends of mine to come? And not even asking me who I want as my best man? You're kidding, aren't you?"

"My father has arranged a best man for you. Sonny something or other."

"Thank God for that. Is there anyone else on my side who's been asked to come? I've got all my mates to think about for the evening do, and even though I haven't got any family left, I'd like to have a few of my close friends at the actual wedding."

*"As I said, it's all been arranged. My father has asked this Sonny person to give him a list of guests on your behalf."*

*"I'll have a word with Sonny, but I'm sure he knows who I'd want. Are we having any bridesmaids or anything, because Sonny's got a daughter. I'm her godfather; I think it's only right I ask her. She's three."*

*"She's our one and only bridesmaid."*

*Relief and anger mingled as one emotion. His life was being directed, and he didn't like it. "Right, I want to get something cleared up now. Where are we going to live? I'm sure it's all been taken care of, because I don't suppose you'd want to go and live at my place."*

*"My father has purchased the house next door. The people who live there unexpectedly said they had to move. A shame, as they've been there for twenty years or so. They'd told me they weren't planning to go anywhere, but it's surprising how some people change their minds."*

*Cardigan changed their minds more like.*

*He sensed Leona didn't have a clue about how low her father would stoop.*

*"I'm feeling tired. Our little conversation has worn me out, so if you don't mind…" She rose from her seat.*

*Jonathan made a swift exit. Telling himself to keep up the rent payments on his childhood home, he went there and parked, walking down to The Eagle for a much-needed drink.*

He rubbed his head now, the elation at the huge beer order receding. Leona was a weird one, there was no mistake about that. He'd keep to the same plan he already had, of hopefully finding someone he could be himself with.

He carried on with the day's work, producing beer for the consumption of ale drinkers, many of whom were of the criminal fraternity.

# Chapter Fifteen

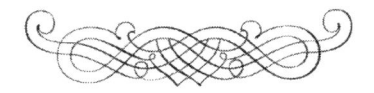

The Brothers were twins and built like garden sheds. Wide frames. They had no qualms about breaking various bones in any unfortunate's body, did as they were told, and were prepared to do most things asked of them in return for a bloody decent wage.

Killing came into the equation, as did robbing, menacing, but any violence directed towards women was immediately frowned upon. No one had been silly enough to ask them to get a woman sorted—not since Mickey Rook asked for his former squeeze to have her face slashed so no other man would look at her. Mickey had received a thump for his trouble, and after visiting the hospital, from which he'd emerged with the knowledge he had a broken jaw, The Brothers let it be known that Mickey was living on borrowed time.

The object of The Brothers' attention was in the process of nosing in his garage. It contained a various assortment of stolen goods, ready for resale to the unsuspecting public, although saying that, some of them were well aware of where the goods came from. The twins, George and Greg Wilkes, watched their target from their battered old Ford van, parked in an alley opposite.

"Cardigan said a broken leg, George."

"Cardigan'll get what he paid for then, won't he."

"We don't want no extras."

"But he's got it coming from us an' all. We can give him what he's due at the same time."

Greg sighed. "He'll think Cardigan arranged for two injuries."

"No, he won't. We'll remind him all about him wanting Shirley Richmond to have a permanent grin. Doing a Cheshire to a woman isn't my style. I wonder if he'll want one for himself. See how he likes it."

"Do it another time. Just do Cardigan's job for now."

"What's up with you? Gone soft on me? We're not going to be able to get hold of him for love nor money once we've broken his leg. He'll go into hiding. It's now or never."

Greg wouldn't be able to change his brother's mind. George was the more stubborn of the two, the stronger half of what they felt were the same person. "Well, I'll leave the talking to you. I suppose you want to smash his leg with the mallet an' all, don't you?"

George laughed. "I wouldn't mind, but seeing as though you don't sound enamoured at doing it, I'll smack his leg one, and when he's down on the floor, I'm going to give him such a happy-looking face, that whoever finds the silly bastard'll think he's enjoying the pain he's in."

"I wonder who'll find him?" Greg said.

"I don't give a toss. That garage isn't left unattended for long. Don't forget, Fartarse

Findley comes by every day with a cargo of goods about half five. That should leave a few hours of unimaginable pain before he's found."

"Fartarse doesn't deliver on a Monday," Greg reminded him.

"What a shame."

"You're a hard sod."

"As far as I'm concerned, we're one and the same, so that makes you just as bad as me. Hold up, he's making a move."

Sighing again and picking up the mallet, Greg glanced at his brother. A large carving knife nestled down the inside of his boot as he got out of the van.

*Shit.*

They mooched over to the garage casually, their prey in the process of locking up. He turned to face his visitors.

"Mickey, my old son. Fancy bumping into you again. How've you been?" George asked.

"All right, Brothers? I haven't seen you two in my face since you busted my jaw. Something up?"

"You should know all about that. We're here on a job, if you get my meaning," George said.

The blood drained from Mickey's face.

"I see you *do* get my meaning then. Now then…" George turned to his twin and held out his hand to receive the mallet. "Cardigan thinks you've crossed him, and we're inclined to agree. Even if we didn't, it pays the rent, doesn't it?" He sniggered.

Mickey shook.

"Cardigan must have been in a good mood, because our instructions were mild. He wants his money back and wasn't happy at all about the stunt you pulled at the poker game the other night. Apparently, you had some money stashed down your trousers that you didn't declare at the beginning. What a naughty boy."

"Bloody hell," Mickey spluttered. "Tell Cardigan he doesn't need to hurt me. I'll drop the money round later. Just let me get the dosh, and I'll meet him wherever he wants."

"It's too late for that. Cardigan thought you might've had a change of heart before he called on us, but seeing as though you're only shitting your pants about the money now, I reckon he'd be angrier still if we didn't carry out his request. How stupid can you get? You know Cardigan isn't someone you can piss about with."

Appealing to Greg's quieter nature, Mickey pleaded, "Come on, fair's fair. I'm telling you, I'll go and pay up straight away. You two can come with me, if you like."

"Fair's fair? Shut your fucking face," George snarled.

Greg stepped forward, as per plan, and grabbed Mickey around the throat, pinning him against his garage door, his feet dangling a few inches from the ground.

"Comfortable, are we?" George asked. "Then let us begin."

Mallet in his fist, he swung it to the side, round and round, the weapon coming close to Mickey's face each time it arced past.

Greg stared at Mickey's feet and let out a loud laugh. A puddle formed on the concrete. "He's a lightweight, George. He's only gone and pissed himself." He kept a firm grip around Mickey's neck.

Mickey's face puffed up, his skin plum-coloured.

"You fucking baby. We aren't cleaning up your mess. We're here to make sure we make some more," George said, still swinging the mallet. "Seeing that you're suitably upset, I won't dilly-dally about any longer. You're nothing but a poxy shitbag who belongs in a nipper's nappy."

Mickey held his breath and shut his eyes — eyes that looked no more than slits. The mallet came down in one final swoop, connecting with Mickey's shin. A sickening thud sounded, and

Mickey's trouser leg, along with his skin, ripped open from a broken bone, numerous shards of marrow dotted about on the flesh.

Mickey screamed. With a nod from George, Greg let him fall in a heap on the cement, slumped against his garage door.

"You've got twenty-four hours from the moment of impact to return Cardigan's money. Let's go, George." Greg was anxious to get away before his brother did any more damage.

George was having none of it. "Rook, there's another matter that needs seeing to, and this time you've pissed *me* off. I warned you that I'd have you when you wanted Shirley Richmond cut, and you must've thought getting your jaw smashed in was punishment enough. It would have been, but I reckon you got her sorted by some other source, and you can tell them we'll find out who they are an' all. But first, I'll deal with the one who wanted it done, *you*, and then you can show them what they've got to come." Giving Mickey a snide look, as he'd dared to open his eyes now, George went down on his haunches in front of him and reached into his boot. "Like the thought of people having a smile for the rest of their lives, do you? Like the thought of hurting women? Well, let's see how it feels, shall we, to have done to you what you ordered for poor Shirley."

"I didn't do it. Someone must have taken it out of my hands."

"And you did nothing to stop him. That makes you just as bad as him in my book. Doesn't this knife gleam? Lovely, isn't it? Cuts through steak like you wouldn't believe. Should make short work of your face, which is a shame, because I really wanted to draw it out, but you know you don't get a nice clean line when you take your time about it. Once your stitches come out, we want my handywork to look like an extension of your lips, don't we."

"P-P-please! Don't—"

"Shut it. Now, open your mouth."

Greg stood by, slightly sickened; his brother was going too far. Mickey was about to be sick, and by the state of his face, tears streaming down his cheeks, mucous hanging from his nose, and spittle dribbling down his chin, Rook was frightened out of his wits.

But open his mouth he did.

George laughed. "Shut your gob over the blade. Close your eyes or keep them open, it makes no odds to me—just sit nice and still."

"Like he's going anywhere, George. Give it a rest, will you?" Greg was well aware that when his brother got himself worked up, there was no turning him back to the land of normality and sanity.

George took a deep breath. "Ready…steady…go!"

The knife cut Mickey's face open from ear to ear, the lower half flopping forward over his chin, his bottom teeth and gums bare. Blood dripped from the shorn skin onto his top.

George smiled. "Like I said, cuts like you wouldn't believe. And a nice straight line, too. Just what the doctor ordered. Talking of quacks, you ought to get yourself to see one pretty sharpish. You've got some nasty injuries there." He turned to go.

Greg's stomach churned. Unnecessary violence wasn't his thing.

The Brothers made their way towards their van.

Getting in, George said, "Fucking hell, I've got blood on my suit. Good job I've got my other one back from the cleaners."

"Let's get out of here. You're stark raving bonkers. I want nothing to do with that face malarkey. A broken jaw was enough for me."

"Shut up. I'll treat you to something to eat. Might settle your stomach a bit." George started the engine, pulled the van out of the alley, and drove over to Mickey's crumpled form. He reversed so the vehicle was alongside their victim and wound down the window.

Mickey looked up in torment. "No more. Please…" It sounded garbled on account of his wound.

"I forgot. The doctor's surgery closes at half four, so you'd best be getting down there quick." Roaring off at high speed towards Cardigan's office, George let out a hoot of deranged laughter.

Greg didn't join him. "You're a sarcastic bastard."

George looked over and smiled his cheeky grin. "I know. It's good, isn't it?"

# Chapter Sixteen

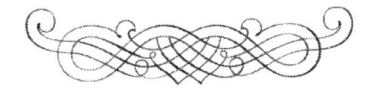

Cardigan slid an envelope across his highly polished desk, caught by the swift action of George Wilkes.

"I'll contact you shortly when I need you again. Got any other jobs on that I might interrupt?" Cardigan asked.

George shook his head. "Nothing we can't put off for you. By the way, I did a little business myself with Rook. He'll be smiling for the rest of his natural, if you know what I mean. I'll take the rap for that, if it doesn't sit well with you."

"You took your time, didn't you? I'd have thought you'd have got him back properly for that Shirley lark ages ago. Thinking about it, I should have done it myself, seeing as she's one of my girls. D'you want me to take the rap or d'you want that one for yourself?"

"Whatever suits you."

Opening his desk drawer with a small key, Cardigan brought out a cash box. He took out a wad of notes and split it in half. "Will two thousand each do you? I'll fork out for the extras. Don't want people thinking I don't pay my way."

George stepped forward to claim his pay, but Greg didn't.

"My money not good enough for you all of a sudden, Greg?" Cardigan peered at him through slitted eyes, testing the big bloke's character, wondering if he'd break under scrutiny.

"Your money's good, but the extra job was George's work. I just stood and watched. I don't want you paying me for something I didn't do."

"Admirable. I like transparency, and no one could accuse you of not being honest. Right…"

Cardigan put Greg's money back in the cash box. "Nice to have done business with you. I'll be in contact."

He moved to the window and watched The Brothers leave his office and swagger to their van. He waited until they'd driven out of sight and turned to Sam. "That Greg's going soft. We'd better watch him. I don't want any cockups where my needs are concerned. On the other hand, George is getting worse. Best we keep him for the really big jobs in future."

"Greg won't do the overly nasty jobs, Ron, and the two always work together. You can't hire one without the other."

"George likes his money, my friend. We'll use them for frightening Pembrooke's potential customers, make Greg think he's off the hook on the big jobs. George'll get bored then and jump at the chance to have a killing. I tell you, there'll be a war now Rook's been sorted, so we'll have to keep our wits about us and have those twins on hand."

# Chapter Seventeen

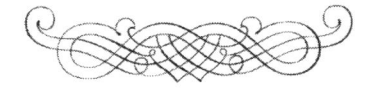

Rebecca laughed loud and hearty as she read the announcement page of the local paper. Leona Cardigan, married. Who on earth this Jonathan Pembrooke was, to have married such a sour old cow, she didn't know, but she found it amusing all the same. She'd have to make it her business to find out who the poor man was and give him her condolences. He was probably as ugly as Leona.

*The one thing I hadn't wanted to happen to Leona — marriage. Damn it.*

Something else would have to be done to ensure Leona's downfall, and Rebecca intended to make it happen.

She poured a cup of tea from her white china pot with its hand-painted pink flowers, then stirred in some sugar using a solid silver spoon, creating a small eddy on the surface. She looked down into the swirling liquid and pictured all sorts of hideous things that could happen to Leona Cardigan. Or Pembrooke, as she'd now be known.

Gracie entered the room, startling her out of her thoughts.

"What are we going to see at the theatre tonight?" she asked. "I didn't quite catch what you said earlier."

"Just a talent contest. It'll raise money for one of the charities I help with, and I thought I'd better show my face to give them my support. Some of the acts are people I know and help."

"Dad would have been impressed at what you do." Gracie smiled.

"Yes, he would." Rebecca had devoted most of her time to helping others, having been shown the other side of the coin by William. She took a moment to compose herself. "I've never told you this before, but it's me who owns the shelter. I've put a lot of money into it already, so now it's down to fund-raising, unless we hit rock bottom, that is. I'll put some more of my own money in then."

"Why didn't you ever say?"

"Because this way, nobody knows, and just think, if the people who use the shelter know I own it and feed them every day, they won't feel as free as they do to talk to me. Go and get ready."

# Chapter Eighteen

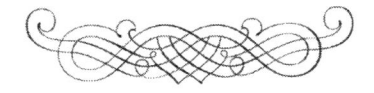

Jonathan and Sonny walked towards that night's venue.

"I never thought it'd be this easy to get out and about after marrying Leona. I thought she'd keep me on a tight rein, but it seems she doesn't mind me going to the boozer, or anywhere else for that matter."

"Of course she doesn't mind you going to your old local," Sonny said. "It's owned by her father, you daft sod. Anything you do'll be reported back, so she hasn't got anything to worry about, has she?"

"I wish she did have something to worry about. This celibacy lark is killing me—not that I'd do it with her if we were the last people on earth." Jonathan laughed, even though the lack of having a bird tormented him.

Arriving at the theatre, they entered the building.

"Be serious now, Sonny. We're here for a good cause. Leona went on and on at me to come, and because she's got a bad cold, she couldn't make it. Thank fuck."

He moved forward on the red carpet and glanced at his surroundings. The foyer had burgundy walls, wood panelling halfway up from the floor in rich mahogany, and a white ceiling with gold coving. Pictures in frames lined the top half, showing who'd played at the theatre and what they'd performed in.

He stepped up to the hosts.

The eldest woman said, "I hope you enjoy the evening." She held out her hand. "Rebecca Lynchwood. And you are?"

Sonny smiled. "Sonny Bates, and this is Jonathan Pembrooke."

The woman's eyes widened a fraction. "Jonathan Pembrooke. How nice to meet you. And you, too, Mr Bates."

Shaking her hand, Jonathan looked up at Rebecca. She appeared somewhat shaken but quickly hid her feelings behind a winning smile.

She turned to her left. "This is my daughter, Gracie."

Jonathan's world turned upside down. Heart hammering, he was at a loss for words. Seconds passed. He glanced from Gracie to Rebecca, who seemed pleased with herself. He returned his gaze to Gracie. She was beautiful and everything he wanted in a woman. He was helpless, realising the enormity of what his life had become, trapped in a marriage with a wife he didn't love, unable to do anything about it.

A queue had formed behind them.

Rebecca said, "I hope you don't think me rude but, Jonathan, would you mind if I nipped to the ladies' room? Would you take my place with Gracie until I came back?"

Mind? Nah, he didn't mind.

Sonny smiled. "I'll go and find our seats, mate."

Jonathan nodded, and Rebecca disappeared, leaving him alone with Gracie to greet the straggle of people who remained in the queue.

---

Rebecca all but skipped to the toilets. Elated she'd found the best way possible at getting back at Leona Cardigan, she laughed and rubbed her hands together.

A question screeched through her mind: *What's a man like him doing married to an old hag of a wretch like Leona?* A puzzle, she had to admit, but one she'd solve, given time. Surely he'd been drunk when he'd proposed.

Rebecca shook her head. Her questions would have to remain unanswered for the time being. There was no way she was going to let this opportunity slip by. This was the moment she'd been waiting to happen for many a long year. Praying for.

*I'm going to hurt you so badly, Leona.*

She took a deep breath and held her head high. Was Leona supposed to have been with Jonathan this evening?

*How would I have reacted to greeting that nasty bitch in the foyer?*

The theatre-goers had come and gone to their seats. Jonathan seemed shy with Gracie, although she didn't understand why, and when he spoke, he reminded her of her dad.

"Shall I stand with you until your mum gets back?" he asked.

"I shouldn't think she'll be very long; she'll want to be getting to our box."

Mum was upon them then and looked at Jonathan. "Listen, why don't you join us in our box? It seems such a waste to hog it all to ourselves."

"Cheers," he said. "I'll go and get Sonny. Which box are you in? We'll come up and find you."

"Number two." Mum smiled. "But we'll wait for you, if you don't mind. I wouldn't want you to get lost."

Jonathan disappeared into the theatre, and Mum turned to Gracie, who smiled, staring in the direction he'd gone.

"Like our Mr Pembrooke, do we?" Mum asked.

"Is it that obvious?"

"Sonny, we've got ourselves a box to sit in."

"Would it be with Gracie and her mum by any chance?"

"It would. Come on, they're waiting for us in the lobby."

"Hold your bloody horses. These seats are so cramped together my legs are stuck. There's no rush; the show doesn't start for another five minutes."

"Of course there's a bloody rush. We're wasting time poncing about in here."

Sonny snorted. "God, he's finally met someone decent. I must say, if I didn't have my missus—"

"Hands off. I saw her first."

"But you're a married man." Sonny pulled at his wedged foot.

"Shut your face about that. With a bit of luck, Leona will be well off the scene by the time me and Gracie are established."

"You're jumping the gun a bit." Sonny freed his legs, getting funny looks from the other seats' occupants. "Flippin' heck. My shoe's come off. It's stuck down the back of the seat in front."

"I'm going. You can get your shoe out on your own and look like a bloody weirdo doing it. I'm going upstairs. It's box number two."

---

Somehow, Sonny got his bastard shoe out. Face hot from the effort, he hopped up the sloping aisle trying to put it on. He stooped to tie the laces. Once done, he smoothed down his trousers then got going.

The dim corridor upstairs arced around in a semicircle, little lights above each door. He found it hard to get his eyes accustomed to the dark, and, racking his brains to remember which box he was supposed to be finding, he came up with number four. Not bothering to knock, he barged in at speed, gaze on the floor.

"Sorry it took so long, but I had to put my shoe back on. Then I couldn't see in the dark and had to feel my way along the walls. Not missed much, have I?"

"You'll be missing a lot more if you don't shut up, Sonny boy. I'll poke both your bleedin' eyes out. Sit down if you're staying or go and find the poor unfortunates you're supposed to be with."

Sonny looked up. An unmistakable wide silhouette, one that even in the darkness brooked no argument, loomed before him.

Cardigan.

*What the hell's he doing here?*

Sonny edged his way out of the box, recalling all of a sudden that the one he should have gone into was number two.

---

Sonny burst into the correct box and sat next to Jonathan, panting to get his breath back.

Jonathan leant over and whispered, "What's up, mate? Didn't you get your shoe out?"

Lifting both feet in the dark, Sonny said, "Yeah, see. But there's something I've got to tell you." He lowered his voice to a whisper. "I went in the wrong box. I barged in, and when I looked up, it wasn't you lot sitting there, was it. I felt a right bloody plonker."

Jonathan stifled laughter.

Sonny sniffed. "You won't be bloody laughing when you find out who was in there, I can tell you."

"Don't tell me, the Duchess of Kent or someone like that."

Sonny scrubbed a hand over his chin. "This is serious stuff, and you really ought to listen before the interval, because you don't want to be bumping into the occupants, I'll make a bet on it."

"Who was it?"

"Cardigan."

Jonathan's heart leapt, and he felt sick. Gracie had asked him if he'd go with her to get the drinks in the interval. If he backed out now, it'd put her off him.

"Christ. D'you reckon he came to spy on me? He'll be wondering where I am, especially as you can see our two empty seats down there. I'll have to come clean and say we were with the hosts. I'll tell Leona when I get home, so when he reports back to her that we weren't even here, I can tell her what the show was all about."

"Keep your bloody eyes peeled then, because we're missing it."

They watched in silence until the first half was over. The woman on the stage, in the process of bringing her act to an end, warbled out a tune. Thin and scrawny, she looked like she needed a good meal.

Rebecca got out of her seat. "I'm going to go down to get some drinks. Would you come with me, Sonny? I don't think I can carry it all on my own."

He jumped up.

Jonathan breathed a sigh of relief.

Rebecca took Sonny's arm, marching him out of the box.

"That was planned, I'll be bound," Gracie said.

"You don't mind, do you?"

"Of course not."

Shoving away the thoughts of Leona and his more than unsatisfactory life, Jonathan told himself to act like they didn't exist while he was with this woman. It was the only way he'd be able to keep up the charade of being single and available—the only way he'd meet Gracie again.

Leona seemed a million miles away now.

"I like you," Gracie said.

He was a bit stunned at that. "Same here. I'd hoped we could get to know each other a bit better, but I work all the hours God sends and might not be able to see you much." That sounded a good enough excuse.

He got his phone out, and they swapped numbers.

The door opened. Sonny and Rebecca came back in.

The lights went down again, and Sonny leant towards Jonathan. Prodding him in the ribs, he whispered, "I hope you know what you're getting yourself into. Cardigan'll slay you alive if he ever finds out. Talking of Cardigan, he's gone. Left with Sam and a few others. Word has it he was doing some sort of deal, something about sorting Mickey Rook once and for all if The Brothers don't take the job. Rook hasn't given Cardigan his money back, so he's pissed off."

"How d'you know that?"

"I was earwigging."

Jonathan turned back to the stage. His shoulders sagged. Cardigan was gone, and his attention was on Mickey Rook. Jonathan had heard down The Eagle that Rook had had his leg smashed in, and someone had cut his face open with a carving knife. Blame went to Cardigan automatically. He'd made no bones about the fact he was after Rook's blood. The grapevine thought Rook's mates were out for revenge, and for that small mercy, Jonathan was grateful. Cardigan wouldn't have the time to be keeping such a close eye on him. To ensure he could spend as many hours as possible with Gracie, he'd be telling Leona all about what her father was getting up to. She'd worry herself silly about that instead of questioning him every time he came home.

Another nudge to his ribs halfway through the second act came from his other side. Jonathan turned his head. Rebecca had prodded him, and she slipped him a piece of paper. He took it and put it in the inside breast pocket of his suit jacket, wondering why Gracie's mother would be passing him notes in the darkened space of a theatre box.

---

In the taxi on the way to The Eagle, Sonny was all chatter.

"Bleedin' hell, mate. Trust you to go out for an evening only to find the best-looking woman in London. If this could have been weeks ago, you could've turned Cardigan down flat. Sod's bloody law. Mind you, that wouldn't have solved the money issue and your business going down the pan."

Jonathan didn't bother responding. He stared down at the white slip of paper Rebecca had given him.

Sonny looked over at him. "What's that?"

"Will you give it a rest? I'm trying to take this in."

Jonathan's heart beat wildly. To understand the note, he'd had to read it again, and it had been difficult because the only light available was from the streetlamps that flickered past. The road had many bumps and potholes, and he had to steady his hand to read the jiggling paper.

*Jonathan,*

*I don't wish to alarm you, but I am aware you're married to Leona Cardigan. It's nothing Sonny said. I saw the announcement in the local paper this evening. I didn't have time to read it when I first got it, hence me knowing about your marriage late. I'm more than happy for you to form a relationship with Gracie; however, I'll tell you of my reasons when we meet again. Would it be possible to see you so I can explain a few home truths about your wife? Give me a ring. As you can see, the phone number is at the top of the page.*

*Rebecca*

Jonathan tried to work out the enigma that Rebecca had given him to solve. How did Rebecca know Leona? What had happened for Rebecca to allow a married man to form a relationship with her own daughter? He'd have to phone her as soon as possible. He'd to do it from The Eagle.

Sonny broke him away from his thinking.

"Take what all in? The fact that your head's been turned by some bit of stuff? Don't take it in, mate, just enjoy it while you can. It won't be long before you get caught out anyway."

"Shut it. You don't know what you're on about half the bleedin' time, and if you took the hint when someone tells you they need a bit of peace and quiet, you'd get along better."

"Sod you then. I was only trying to cheer you up."

"I know." Jonathan sighed. He loved Sonny, but sometimes he didn't know when to give it a rest.

The taxi came to a halt outside The Eagle, and he leapt out.

"I'll pay then, shall I," Sonny said sarcastically and handed the driver some change.

# Chapter Nineteen

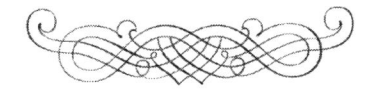

Debbie sat at the bar in The Angel with her usual Coke, leaving Lavender to man the parlour reception desk. She was waiting for Shirley to come in—she was starting later tonight. She'd messaged to ask if they could have a chat before work. She wouldn't say what it was about, stating it was better face to face.

God, was she going to jack her job in after all? That wasn't an issue, filling her slot in the parlour, Debbie had a waiting list with several girls on it, but she'd hate to lose her friend. She brightened her nights and sometimes her days when they got together in the afternoons.

Debbie caught a glimpse of herself in the mirror behind the bar and smiled at her reflection. She'd gone and visited the salon earlier, getting her hair done like she wanted. A million quid, that was what she felt like, and it had given her a boost. She couldn't wait for Cardigan to see it.

Shirley appeared in the mirror, a hand on each of the double doors where she'd pushed them open. Her short red skirt was making friends with her knickers, and a black crop top exposed her toned belly. Hair in messy bun — Debbie knew how it got in the way when you bent over to give a punter a blow job — she'd done her face up nice, and if you didn't know she'd been cut, from here it looked like her skin was scar-free.

She walked towards Debbie, and a man reached out to slap her arse.

"That's a fiver," Shirley said, stopping with her hand out.

"It was just a tap, Shirl."

"I don't give a toss. Money."

He fished his wallet out and removed a tenner. "Here." Then he slapped her bum again.

She snatched the cash and stuffed it in her handbag, trotting up to Debbie and taking a perch. "Did you bloody see that?"

"Yep."

"Cheeky bastard. Well, that taught him. He won't do it anymore if he has to fork out for it. Lemonade, Lisa, please."

"He's the sort who thinks he can touch just because of what you do for a living." Debbie would have a word with him later, tell him to watch himself or she'd get shirty.

"Exactly that."

"What did you want to talk about?" Debbie drank some Coke.

"Hang on. Let me get my drink first, then we can go in the parlour. This needs to be said in private."

*Shit, she's really going to leave.* "All right."

They sat quietly until Lisa brought the lemonade over, and Debbie told her to put it on her tab. She led the way, pushing past a couple of blokes chatting outside the men's, then into the corridor. She unlocked the parlour door, her tummy going over about what was to come. She'd try to persuade her friend to stick around but wouldn't push it if Shirley was adamant.

In the reception area, they sank onto a sofa each, Debbie sending Lavender off to her room so they had privacy.

"Come on then, out with it." Debbie cradled her Coke. If she smoked, she have a fag she was that nervous.

"Something happened last night when I left here."

A pinch of guilt nipped Debbie at feeling relieved. Then worry overtook it. "What?"

"I was walking home, and you know by the cemetery?"

"Yeah…"

"Someone dragged me inside the tree tunnel."

Debbie's guts contracted. "Did they hurt you?"

Shirley shook her head. "No, thank God. Well, not like you mean. I got scuffed heels where he'd carted me along."

"Fuck your shoes. I'll buy you a new pair."

"Not those heels, you silly tart. My actual feet."

"Ow."

"Yeah, they're a bit sore."

"So what happened?"

Shirley sipped some lemonade, probably to stall. She'd done this when Debbie had grilled her after she'd been cut. Got all cagey, staring at the ceiling like she was doing now. "He wanted to say sorry."

Debbie shot forward, her drink nearly spilling. "Oh, fucking hell. Vinny."

"Yep."

"What did you say?"

"Nothing. I was too worried about what he'd do. Anyway, he said if he says sorry, that makes it okay until next time."

"I knew he was a fucking abuser."

"He wants me to ask you if he can come back here."

"I bet he bloody does, and the answer's no."

"Good. He gives me the creeps." Shirley shivered.

"Want me to get hold of Cardigan?"

"Nah, I'll wait and see if Vinny bugs me again."

"Best he doesn't drag you anywhere a second time, otherwise The Brothers will go after him. You know what they're like about that sort of thing."

With the plan settled, they nattered about the storm and how it'd taken them both ages to get to sleep. Debbie wondered whether Shirley had stayed awake for another reason altogether. Like seeing Vinny again in the dark tree tunnel.

It was enough to invite insomnia in for a place to stay.

# Chapter Twenty

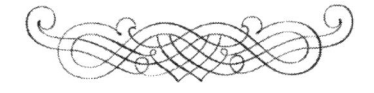

Rebecca's mobile rang.
"I have to take this, Gracie." She walked into the lounge and shut the door. "Hello?"

"It's Jonathan. Sorry to bother you so late. Can we meet tomorrow?"

"Yes, I go to mass in the morning, but other than that…"

"Where?"

"My church. It's the one down by the large park near where we live." She gave her address.

They arranged a time. Rebecca cut the call and slid her phone in her bag. She was meeting him straight after church, in the graveyard behind the big clock tower. She'd make Leona out to be so hideous he'd want to get away from her fast.

She went into the kitchen.

Gracie was spooning sugar and cocoa into their large mugs. "Who was that on the phone at this time of night?"

"Just someone who wants to know more about the charity. I said I'd meet him after mass. No need for you to go so early, I know you've had a tiring week."

*Please don't insist on coming.*

Gracie smiled. "Good, because I'll probably give church a miss altogether."

Rebecca sighed inwardly. The mission was a go.

# Chapter Twenty-One

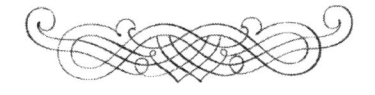

Leona was propped up in bed, sniffling into her lace-edged handkerchief, her eyes watering and her nose sore. She'd wiped it so many times she'd chafed the skin.

She'd wanted to go to the theatre this evening, not to watch the acts but to see Rebecca again. What a shocker it would've been for Rebecca to see her, plain Leona, on the arm of a younger man. But instead she was stuck at home, left to her own devices while her husband went out and enjoyed himself. He'd said he was taking that friend of his, Sonny.

More than a little sorry for herself, she picked up her magazine, but the words merged into one another, and she could hardly concentrate. Her thoughts wandered, and she ruminated over the past couple of weeks.

The wedding itself had gone by without a hitch, except for Jonathan's guests, who were loud. A short weekend break served as a honeymoon. That had been stilted and uncomfortable to say the least, and she sensed he knew he'd made the biggest mistake of his life. They'd hardly spoken, except for polite conversation and common courtesy. The hotel receptionist had looked at them strangely when they'd arrived. She'd handed over two sets of keys for their separate rooms.

As they'd walked away from the desk, she'd muttered, "No wonder they've got two rooms. Who'd want to get in bed with that?"

Leona wasn't stupid. The woman had referred to her, and it had hurt.

The move into the new house hadn't been so bad. Her father had bought all the furniture for them, and it'd been delivered while they'd been away. Leona just took her personal possessions and clothes, and Jonathan arrived with a suitcase, its contents unknown.

She hardly saw him. He was a sullen and moody man. She let him out and about, though. Her father's men would keep a close eye on him. He went to work and came home, often going out with that Sonny, coming home around eleven. With a grunt of goodnight, he went to his room, and the next day began and ended exactly the same way.

Weekends weren't much different, so she could say she'd got what she'd asked for really. A marriage in name only. She was still niggled, though. She'd envisaged candlelit meals, chats over coffee, some sort of warmth and togetherness. Just because they weren't having sex, didn't mean they couldn't forge some sort of bond. It just seemed to her he wanted nothing but to honour his promise to her father.

Sighing, she got up and went down to the kitchen, intending to make herself a hot drink to help relax her. Milk in the pan, she jumped at the sound of the front door opening then closing. The kitchen door swung open, and in breezed Jonathan, who for once didn't scowl at her.

"Couldn't you sleep?" he asked.

"No." Leona sniffed. A bit of sympathy wouldn't go amiss.

"Oh, well, make your milk, and maybe you'll feel better."

It couldn't be alcohol that had him in such a good mood. He rarely had more than three pints—her father had said so after asking Jack at The Eagle.

"Did you enjoy yourself?" She added a sniffle at the end of her sentence to elicit some kind of caring response.

"Yeah, we had a great time. The host let us share her box, said she knew you from years ago."

"You shared a box with Rebecca Lynchwood?" Leona's sniffles and sneezes were forgotten.

"Yeah, she seems quite a nice woman—"

"You don't know her. She's the one who stole my William away from me. Did she say anything else about me?"

"Only that she knew you, that's all. What are you getting in such a fix about?"

"I'm not. How did you come to be talking about me?" She whittled her handkerchief.

"She said she'd seen our wedding announcement in the paper. Anyway, I'm off to bed. I'm out early in the morning."

"On a Sunday? May I ask where you're going?"

"You can ask, but I'm not telling you." He left the kitchen.

Leona seethed in his wake.

*That Rebecca always gets the better of me. Why does everything I plan go wrong? And why is he in such a good mood? I bet he's got a thing for her.*

With those thoughts in mind, she splashed the milk into her cup, added some sugar, and made her way to bed. She walked past Jonathan's room. He sang, which only served to confirm her suspicions. Rebecca had succeeded in taking something away from her. Again.

She went to her room, livid. Jonathan's rudeness returned to taunt her. How dare he say she could ask where he was going but he didn't have to tell her.

# Chapter Twenty-Two

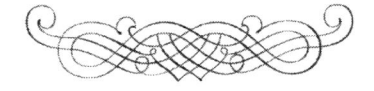

Jonathan waited behind the church at half eight. The day would heat up in no time, and the dew would soon evaporate, leaving the grass dry enough to walk on without getting the toes of his shoes wet.

He couldn't go anywhere without thinking he was being followed. The uneasiness, together with the hairs rising on the back of his neck, convinced him that people had been told to keep an eye out and report back. All he did was go to the pub with Sonny most nights. There were no women involved.

Until now.

Gracie had him feeling happy and sad at the same time. Happy he had something to look forward to, and sad she only served to show him what Leona was really like: old, his jailer from now until whenever he set himself free.

He could hardly believe he'd only met Gracie last night, having got on so well with her. He felt like he'd known her for years instead of hours. What a shame she couldn't be his properly, what with Leona in the shadows.

He imagined all their future furtive meetings, going places where they wouldn't be seen by Cardigan or one of his watchmen. How would he explain to her, should she want to go somewhere on The Cardigan Estate, that he'd rather not, without sounding odd or suspicious? Would Rebecca help him out with that? Her note had made it clear she didn't mind the idea of him seeing her daughter, even though she knew he was married. Only time would tell on that score. He'd have to talk to her about that.

Sitting on the bench provided for mourners, he looked down at the path and wondered again what she wanted to talk about regarding Leona. He suspected he'd hear a different story to Leona's. What was the feud between them really about? Whose story would he believe? He hardly knew either woman.

He yawned and put his hand up to cover his mouth. Rebecca came towards him. Immaculately dressed in a long beige coat, the ends of her pretty cream shawl flapped in the breeze as she drew level with him.

"Good morning. Shall we walk?" she asked.

He got up and greeted her warmly then strode beside her down the path leading to the vast cemetery. She seemed to know where she was going, and after walking in silence for a short while, they came to a halt by the graveside of William Lynchwood.

She gazed down at the headstone. "I loved him with all my heart, you know. Still do. I wish every day that things could have turned out differently, but every morning I wake up and it's all the same. I'm alone, and he's still dead. Life's unfair, and I never want Gracie to have to go through what I have. You like her, don't you?"

Jonathan cleared his throat. "Yeah. I want you to know that once I can get out of my marriage, I'll be able to be with her properly."

"How did you get yourself into that situation? If you don't mind me asking, that is."

Jonathan took a deep breath. It wouldn't do any good to lie, especially when he wanted to form a permanent relationship with her daughter. He'd tell her the lot, all about Cardigan and the card game, whether she thought it distasteful that he was a gambling man or not.

After his tale, Rebecca shook her head. "I can guess what the deal was, but go on, tell me."

Her sympathetic manner put him at ease, and in the quiet surroundings he was able to carry on.

Once he'd finished, she said, "Leona isn't the nicest woman, is she."

"The way she puts on that posh accent of hers really gets on my wick." He paused and ground his teeth in anger. "The wedding was all right. I was able to get drunk and blot it all out, but since then I've hardly been able to look at her. I'm bound to her for God knows how long, and it makes me sick to my stomach." He rubbed his face with both hands.

"You don't plan to stay with her, do you?"

Jonathan wanted to laugh. "Even before I met Gracie last night, I wanted to get rid of Leona.

Cardigan orders my beer now, and it's fine while he's doing that. I can keep afloat and have plenty of cash to spare, but once I leave Leona, he'll withdraw the orders. I signed something to that effect. I need to build up custom elsewhere, but I tell you, whoever I approach just doesn't want to know."

"Cardigan might have something to do with that. If he wants you to stay with his daughter, of course he'll put off any other customers."

"It's just one of those things. Everyone gets to hear that you're going downhill, and they go to someone else. I reckon I need to branch out a bit, tout for business farther afield."

Rebecca nodded and eyed the grass. "Look, let me tell you the reasons why I don't mind you seeing my daughter. You can't let Leona come between you. I will say, for the record, that if Gracie ever finds out you're married, I'll deny all knowledge of it to protect our relationship. Is that clear?"

"Yeah, I can understand that. I wouldn't expect you to do anything else. I don't want her to find out I've ever been married until it's all over and I'm free."

"That would be best." She went on to tell him of her past. "So you can imagine my surprise when I saw your announcement in the paper. I imagined you to be just as old as she is. When your friend introduced you at the theatre… I thought you must have married her for Cardigan's protection. I had no idea it could be something like this."

"Me seeing Gracie would give you some sort of satisfaction then, especially if it came to something and we stayed together?"

"Yes, I have my own interests at heart on that score, but ultimately my daughter's welfare is my main objective, so if you make her unhappy, I'll have something to say about it."

"As you have every right to. It's just a matter of sorting out this Leona business."

"It'll all come out in the wash, you'll see."

"Got something up your sleeve?"

"I might have. Would you like to come back to our house? We can tell Gracie I bumped into you on the way home."

"I was going to ring her once I'd left you anyway."

"Well, that saves you having to, doesn't it?"

---

Gracie had been on edge all morning. She'd finally fallen asleep around three a.m. and woke again at nine. Getting dressed and going down for breakfast, she'd waited for her phone to ring.

She sat at the kitchen table in a daydream, finding it hard to believe she'd met a man the night before—and she hadn't even been looking for him.

Her last boyfriend had been all sweetness and light when they were in company, and angry and selfish while they were alone. She'd ended their relationship in a crowded pub—he wouldn't make a scene in public. He'd called her for days afterwards, nice at first, and then the phone calls got nasty, until she threatened him with the police. The calls stopped, and she'd seen him out on a few occasions with her friends from the office. He hadn't approached her or acted like he knew her in any way.

Her stomach was in knots every time she thought of Jonathan and remembered the sound of his voice. She idly flicked through the Sunday newspaper on her phone, seeing the pages but not taking in what was happening in the world.

Her mother's key slid in the lock, and she entered the house chatting animatedly. "She'll be so pleased to see you."

*She's brought someone back from church.*

"Gracie? Are you out of bed yet?" Mum called.
"I'm in the kitchen."

"Are you decent before we come in, because I've brought home a guest."

"Yes, I'm decent."

Mum walked in the kitchen. Gracie didn't look up from her phone but sighed, ready to put on an act for five minutes or so then she'd escape to her room.

"Perhaps I can cheer her up?"

Gracie's stomach turned over. "What are you doing here?"

"Not welcome then? I got the impression last night…"

"I didn't expect it to be you."

"I'll leave you to it," Mum said. "I've got some letters to write, and they're rather pressing."

She left the kitchen. As soon as the door closed, Gracie got up, wound her hands around Jonathan's neck, and kissed him.

---

Jonathan chose a pub on the outskirts, far enough away from their patch not to be recognised. They went in Gracie's car, and he kept a strict eye out to make sure they hadn't been followed. They hadn't—not by a particular old white van belonging to The Brothers anyway—and he relaxed.

In the bar, they had a drink, talking as if it were second nature to be sitting together as a new couple. The time slipped by quickly, and before he knew it, the barman had come over and told them if they wanted food, they'd better make their way to the eating area.

No one else occupied the restaurant section, and Jonathan talked freely with no pressure from the bar staff to hurry. Later, he paid for their meals, and they left The Jack of Hearts. He looked up at the sign which was a picture of a playing card. Leona and that damn poker game would always be there in the back of his mind, but he quickly shoved the thought away. No need to think about his other life; he still had a couple of hours to go in Gracie's company yet.

Not wanting to drive home, he suggested a walk. He steered her down the lane beside the pub to see where it led. Open fields spread before them, and they tromped across one, chatting all the while. Holding hands, they appeared like any other couple, only that wasn't true.

Over the way was another field, and, climbing over the stile, they jumped into it. Cows stood at the other end. Gracie sat and leant back on her palms, while Jonathan sprawled flat on his back, putting his hands under his head.

"Next time we should bring a picnic basket," Gracie said.

"Oh, so you reckon there's a next time then?"

"Why wouldn't there be?"

Jonathan stiffened. "No reason."

"We have nothing to worry about, do we?"

Why had she asked that? "No, nothing at all." Guilt soured his gut.

"What's wrong?" she asked, her frown deep.

"Nothing."

They went further than a kiss in the long grass. Later, chewing a blade of grass, Jonathan propped himself up on one elbow, looking down at her.

"My place isn't much. It was my mum's before she died. There's a few sticks of furniture, so we can go there if you don't mind slumming it."

"Sounds perfect."

"We'd better go," he said, conscious of how long he'd been out.

They walked to the pub car park, and Gracie made the suggestion of another drink.

Jonathan nodded. "Yeah, but then I really have to get back. I've got a busy day tomorrow."

In The Jack of Hearts, he paid for their drinks and glanced up at the clock on the wall behind the bar. Half seven. Leona would be wondering what he'd been doing all this time. He'd have to think of an excuse on the way home. Calculating when he'd eventually arrive—they had to drive back to Gracie's and then he'd planned to walk from there—he'd have Leona's suspicions aroused, unless he said he'd been at the office all day, despite it being Sunday.

Drinks finished, they left the pub.

In the car, Gracie said, "I'll drop you home. Then I'll know where to come."

Thinking fast, he told her his old address. He'd drop in at The Eagle and show his face, so at least someone had seen him throughout the day. He gave Gracie the directions, and they arrived in no time. She leant over to his seat to give him a goodbye kiss. Nervous of being spotted, he returned it then leapt out of the car, cursing himself for losing his cool. He gave her a peck on the cheek then closed the door.

Remembering he was meant to have met Sonny at twelve.

*Fuck.*

# Chapter Twenty-Three

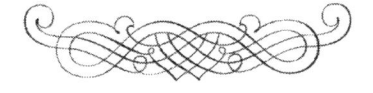

Harry 'Fartarse' Findley needed to speak to Mickey urgently, and, not having found him at their usual haunts, he drove to the garage to check if he was there.

"What the fuck is that?"

A figure lay hunched in the light of his headlamps.

He swerved his car and parked, then ran to the figure he hardly recognised as Mickey. Face open to the elements, teeth bared, Mickey looked a right old fucking mess.

"Jesus Christ." Harry heaved.

Mickey's damaged leg lay sprawled in front of him, the other tucked beneath. Harry pulled out his phone and dialled a number he knew off by heart. "Fucking hell, get down here quick. Rook's had his face slashed open. No, I'm not pissing you about, I mean it."

"Who did that?" the person said.

"Fuck knows, but when I find out, they're dead."

Mickey stirred.

Harry shoved his phone away and knelt, putting his hand on his friend's shoulder. "It's all right, mate. It's me, Harry. How long have you been here? And who the fucking hell did this?"

Mickey shook his head as if to clear it and winced. "Broth... Br..."

It was all Harry needed to know.

Then Mickey spoke again, only fainter this time. "Card..."

*Those fucking twins and Cardigan.*

Thank God help would soon be here in the form of a bent doctor who'd gladly set Mickey's leg and sew up his face.

For a sum.

# Chapter Twenty-Four

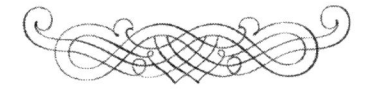

It was July, and Mickey recuperated in a safe house. Harry had made the decision to sort Cardigan in return for what he'd done to Mickey, and they'd devised a plan. It was risky, messing with Cardigan, but the bloke had gone too far, and someone needed to stand up to him. Mickey wouldn't get the blame for this, as the less-than-law-abiding doctor from another estate had assured Findley he'd vouch that Mickey Rook couldn't have committed any crime in this state. All he was capable of was sitting in pain. And that was a crime to Mickey. He liked to be out and about.

"I'm going to have him," Harry said, vehement, scrunching his eyes into slits.

Even though Harry was thin and darted about all over the place, hence the nickname Fartarse, Mickey wouldn't want to meet him as an enemy in a dark alley.

Mickey was near enough his old self. "Just be careful, that's what I think. You can't take Cardigan on alone. He's always got that limpet, Sam, with him. You'll never be able to do it."

"I'm just waiting on the geezer who gets the guns. I don't have to be anywhere near the bloke to kill him. Get my drift?"

"Right, I'm with you. I thought you were just going to rough him up a bit. What about the twins? What are you planning to do about them?"

"I don't know yet. They were only carrying out orders, weren't they?"

"No. They said my smile was a present from them. Because of that Shirley thing. I thought they'd forgotten all about it."

"They're like elephants in mind as well as body then, because they obviously didn't forget; they were just biding their time. Crafty fuckers." Harry shook his head.

"Well, I'll leave it up to you, but didn't someone say Cardigan paid them for my face? Perhaps they were just acting big when they said it was their doing."

"We'll give them the benefit of the doubt this time," Harry said, "but if we hear any different in the future, we'll have them sorted."

"Do what you like. I'm thinking of getting out of London. It's getting a bit too hairy for me. I'm tired of it all...and a bit scared, though I wouldn't let on to anyone but you."

"Shut your face, Mickey. We're a team. Always have been and always will be. Don't go deserting me when we've got our fingers in so many pies. We can make a bleedin' packet if we hold on long enough."

Mickey sighed and closed his eyes. His leg was sore and itched like mad beneath the plaster cast—still, it'd be coming off soon. His face was stiff where he'd talked too much. "We can't do the market stalls and the door-to-door sales pitch anymore with the hooky gear. Or wait for the big boys to ask for some stuff and have them on our backs while we're trying to nick it for them. We need to break into the big time, or I tell you, I'm moving on."

"I'll get something arranged. Don't give up on me, especially while I'm in the process of getting Cardigan done over."

Mickey's head hurt. He let sleep overtake him.

# Chapter Twenty-Five

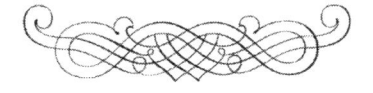

Shirley was sick of Vinny watching her. While she'd successfully avoided him—Iris had been walking her home in the early hours then getting a taxi from Shirley's—she'd seen him standing opposite her flat, wedged in an alley between two houses with a couple of wheelie bins for cover. Except they didn't give him cover, his top half visible in the light of a nearby streetlamp. If he wanted to be surreptitious, he wasn't doing a good job of it.

She was on edge most of the time, and her work was suffering. Despite the CCTV at the parlour door, she kept tormenting herself with images of him turning up and barging in along with a booked client, overpowering Debbie then rushing to Shirley's room and getting lairy with her. She jumped a lot whenever she thought someone was behind her, even in the reception area, and Debbie had noticed.

Now, safe in Debbie's flat, Shirley discussed it with her. "It's just that I need to get a handle on things, that's all. He's so weird, that's the problem. I suppose if he's only watching me, it's doing no harm, but when it's wreaking havoc with my day-to-day life…"

Debbie sighed. "If you don't want Cardigan to do the honours, at least let me have a word with The Brothers. They're not just Cardigan's boys, you know, they work for others. I'd gladly pay them to give him a warning. They're good at breaking legs. At least Vinny won't be able to run after you when you've finished work."

Shirley had been scarred in more ways than one from the cut. *That* man had warned her not to say anything else he'd kill her, and if Vinny got arsey enough, he'd undoubtedly do the same. "Nah, leave it. He'll get bored eventually. Anyway, I need to get home. Got some washing to do. Thanks for the chat."

Hugs given, Shirley walked down the steel steps and sidled to the corner of The Angel. She peered out to make sure no one was about—well, Vinny—then jogged down the street, mindful of keeping an eye out. She rounded the corner and crossed the road—sod walking directly past the cemetery again—and crossed back before she got to the alley Vinny usually loitered in.

She made it to her front door and cursed herself for not taking her keys out of her bag, ready. She knew he was there the moment she curled her fingers around the bunch. Behind her on the steps. She stared at the glass in the communal front door and caught his reflection. He stood to her right, appearing the same height as her even though he was two steps down.

"You've been avoiding me," he said, "and I'm hurt."

Earlier, Debbie had already predicted Vinny was fixated on Shirley, and she'd said, "He's copped an eyeful of your scar and thinks you're vulnerable, easily manipulated."

Shirley couldn't agree more. "Just been busy and haven't seen you about."

He cocked his head as if thinking about whether she'd told the truth. "Hmm. I'll let you off on that one. But how come that Iris has been walking you home?"

"New rules at work," Shirley lied. "We need to go in pairs."

"So why can't *you* walk *her* home, then get a taxi here?"

*Because I'd be alone, you dickhead.* "I don't make the rules."

"Open the door then." He smirked.

She had the urge to kick the reflection of his face, turn and stab him in the eye with a key. "Um—"

"Did you ask Peony about letting me back?"

"Yes."

"What did she say?"

"Maybe go and ask her yourself?"

"I want you to tell me." He clamped a hand on her shoulder.

Shirley held in her fear. He was getting seriously frightening now. As if watching her wasn't enough, he had to do this. Good job it was daylight, or she'd have crapped herself.

A wave of relief went through her—one of the other residents came out of her ground-floor flat and stared at Shirley. Julie. A sex worker. A lifeline.

Shirley pulled a face—*fucking help me!*—hoping Vinny didn't catch it in the glass.

Julie copped on and came to the door, fake smiling. She opened it. "Ah, there you are. I was beginning to think you'd never come back. Are you ready then, or do you need a wee first?"

"Best have a wee." Shirley stepped inside.

Julie shut the door on Vinny and led the way to her place. Inside, Shirley leant against the wall, her body wobbly all over.

"I've seen him down the alley opposite, *and* on the patch," Julie said. "Nearly called the police the other night. I caught him trying to get into the flats."

Shirley's legs went, and she sagged down a bit. "What?"

"I opened my window and told him to fuck off. It was about four in the morning, the twat." Julie bent over to help Shirley upright. "So what's going on? Dodgy punter?"

"Yeah. Peony's stopped him coming to the parlour. He was rude about my face." Shirley touched it self-consciously. "She doesn't hold with shit like that."

"Cheeky bastard. You should ring the police if he's been watching you. What did he want just then?"

"To see if Peony will let him back. I didn't tell him she said no. Thought he might turn nasty."

"Best thing. Come on, let's go and see if he's gone."

"I have to go home. I've got washing to do."

"Fuck the washing. This is more important."

Julie walked off, and Shirley followed her, shaking at the thought of Vinny still being outside. He was down the alley again, actually *sitting* on a wheelie bin.

"He's not right in the head," Julie said.

No, he wasn't, and neither was Shirley if she let this carry on. But what else could she do? If Vinny turned out like her cutter, she'd be dead.

# Chapter Twenty-Six

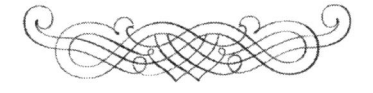

George and Greg waited for Cardigan to arrive. He was coming over to give them their instructions on sorting Mickey once and for all.

Greg was antsy. "Apparently, before he came to us, Cardigan went to someone else to do his dirty work with regards to killing Rook, but they refused. Said what he wanted doing was a step too far. God knows what it is. I don't even know that we ought to do it, because if it's been turned down already, it might be gruesome."

"Greg, you're like a sack of spuds. Don't want to do this job, don't want to do that. What's up with you?" George frowned.

"Cardigan's getting too much like the bleedin' Mafia. One measly slight and he's after your blood. I tell you, I'm pissed off to the back teeth with him. He clicks his fingers, and we come running. Does he think we're scared of him or something? We could knock the old man out, and he wouldn't be able to see for a week. He can't be a hardman if he hasn't got any hardmen."

George snorted. "What're you saying? That we should jack it in?"

"No, just get rid of Cardigan. He's started to get on my nerves."

"He's the main one who pays the bills. We can't get rid of him."

"Of course we can, then we'll take over The Cardigan Estate."

"That's not a bad idea, but I want to do Mickey first."

"Oh, sod you," Greg bit back, downhearted. "I can't get through to you these days. All you seem to want is blood and gore. I bet you'll take this job on without batting an eyelid. Some other fucker's turned it down, and you? You'd take it. There's something wrong with you."

"Shut your bleedin' mush," George snapped. "Cardigan's here."

Greg peered out of the window. Cardigan had indeed turned up, late as usual. Perhaps they should give him a telling off for being tardy. It was all right for Cardigan to be late, but not them.

George opened the door, and Cardigan's big frame swanked into the room, all smiles, his manner chirpy. Sam followed.

*Being fucking amicable to butter us up for the job. Wanker.*

Greg had a gut feeling they should refuse before they even knew what it entailed, but George…

Cardigan clapped. "Right, lads. I've got a proposition for you. How about getting Mickey Rook again? I don't think he got the message last time. Word's out that he's planning to have me done over." He laughed, loud and false. "Now, we all know how silly that is, don't we, but you can't take any chances, can you. What d'you say?"

George looked over at Greg and nodded.

George took the lead. "What d'you want doing? Then we'll let you know if we're prepared to do it."

George must have bad vibes, else he would've accepted the job there and then, not wanting to know any details until the agreement had been signed and the first instalment paid.

"That's unusual for you, George." Cardigan appeared startled.

"I just want to know what it entails first. Isn't a crime, is it?"

"No, but being rude to me is, but I'll do you a favour and let it slip." Cardigan's brow bunched, and his eyes narrowed.

Greg had had enough of this sort of lark.

*How big does Cardigan think he is? No one would touch us if he approached them to do us in. He's living in cloud-cuckoo-land, that one.*

"How gracious of you," George said, rigid shoulders and tight fists indicating his rising anger. "Now, what d'you want doing?"

"Temper, temper." Cardigan paused. "Goes without saying I want you to actually finish Rook off. But first, cut off all his fingers, one by one. Just leave him with the thumbs-up on both hands, like he's in agreement with what's been done. Then, when he's really in pain, you can lop off his cock and bollocks and leave him for a few minutes.

Once he's suffered, you can finish him off any way you like. How's that sound?"

George glanced at Greg.

*I don't want anything to do with this job. But, shit, if George gives the nod, I'll join him whether I like it or not.*

George stared straight at Cardigan. "We'll do it. For a price."

Cardigan smiled. "Name it."

# Chapter Twenty-Seven

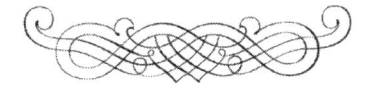

August. Bloody hot.

Vinny, uncomfortable in the heat belting into the alley from the vicious sun directly overhead, got angrier by the minute. How come it was taking so long for Peony to decide whether he could go back to the parlour or not? He wasn't stupid, the answer was no, and Shirley was avoiding telling him—avoiding *him*. He didn't need all his GCSEs to work that one out.

Why didn't she like him? It seemed she didn't anyway. How come she said she'd accepted his apology yet managed to stay far enough away that he could never get near her? Except that day on her steps. Sometimes, he didn't see her leave for The Angel at her usual time, yet when he went there and asked anyone outside at the tables if they'd seen her, the answer was always: "Yep, she's in."

She must be going out the back of the flats.

Someone in her block hadn't changed their routine, though. A bloke with floppy hair, who left about seven in the morning, always got into his black BMW and drove off. Work. That was for losers, having a permanent job. Vinny preferred drifting from building site to building site, cash-in-hand gigs when he felt like it while getting the dole. He was a brickie, and people always needed one of those.

Floppy Hair would be out in a minute, so Vinny ran over the road and stood on the pavement, waiting for the bloke to come down the stairs—he had the second-floor flat, and Vinny was jealous the fella got to hear Shirley moving about upstairs. There he was, so Vinny walked along, smiling.

The man opened the door.

"Hold up," Vinny said. "Leave that open for me. Want to surprise the missus."

"That's what she calls herself, is it?" The bloke waited for Vinny to get to the top of the steps.

"What d'you mean by that?"

"Well, it depends which missus you mean. Both of them are slappers."

Vinny wanted to crush this dick's face, but he needed to keep him amenable. "Those two? Fuck off. I'm with the bird on the fourth floor." Lie.

"Ah." He all but skipped off in his poncy way.

Vinny went inside, up the stairs to the third floor, putting his gloves on. Adrenaline punched through him, and he took a moment to steady himself. This was it.

It didn't take long to open the door with the lockpick. Problem was, Shirley had a chain on, so he'd have to kick his way inside. The woman on the top floor might normally come down to investigate, which wasn't ideal, but her car wasn't out the front, so maybe she'd stayed away last night.

That just left the bitch downstairs, and he'd overheard her telling Shirley as they'd walked to The Angel the other night that she used earplugs while sleeping.

Fate. He loved it.

One swift kick had the door flying inwards, and he stepped inside, closing it and double locking it behind him. If she ran and managed to get this far, she'd be stalled by fiddling with the Yale.

He strode down the narrow hall.

She appeared around a doorjamb, clutching it, her eyes wide. "Oh God…"

"You can call me God if you like, but Vinny'll do."

She disappeared inside the room. He followed, cautious in case she had a weapon. Girls like her must fear for their lives. But it was all right, he had a weapon an' all.

He filled the doorway. There she was, standing beside her double bed, knife pointing his way.

"No need for that, is there?" he asked. "You'll get me ratty if you try using it."

She shivered, and he wondered if his 'voice', the one he'd used when he'd chatted shit about her face, was the catalyst for it.

"Put it down," he said. "No need to get funny. I just thought that if I can't come to the parlour, I can do you here instead. Doesn't matter where, so long as I can see you. I like fucking you."

She dropped the knife on the bed. "Okay…"

"There's a good girl. Now pick it back up again and throw it in the corner. If you lob it at me, I'll stab you." He dug into his pocket and took his penknife out. "With this. Bit of a sharp fucker."

She did as he'd asked, staring at where her knife had landed on a pile of dirty washing. Filthy cow didn't even have a basket for it. That annoyed him, but he could fix that, train her up, and she'd be how he wanted her in no time. Compliant. Only his. Truth be told, that scar turned him on. He imagined *he'd* cut her, not some other lucky bastard, and visualised it every night before he dropped to sleep.

"Get your clothes off," he ordered, using the voice.

She didn't have much to remove, just a pair of flimsy pyjamas—shorts and a little top with thin straps. Pink. She seemed to like that colour if she wasn't at work. He stared at her beauty spot above her top lip. That turned him on an' all. The only thing missing today was her makeup. She usually used thick kohl, and coupled with her black hair, she looked proper slutty, just the way he liked her.

Shirley folded her arms over her big tits.

"Now don't be doing that. I want to see the goods."

She lowered them. "Can you at least let me have a shower first?"

"Nah, I want you dirty." The idea of her sweating all night in bed… Lovely.

"It's the same price as at the parlour." She stared at him, defiance in her eyes.

He'd enjoy beating that out of her.

"I've got the money," he said.

He didn't.

"Right. Get on the bed then."

She shouldn't be bossing him about, she knew that. He'd told her the rules at the parlour. Why was she flouting them?

Anger surged. "You don't get to tell me what to do." He darted at her, shoving her on the bed, landing on top of her. She was so small compared to him, he felt bloody brilliant. Invincible. "I can see your scar better without makeup on." He took a glove off and stroked the knobbly line from one side to the other, her lips a softer touch between.

She went rigid.

"That's it, go stiff, I like it," he whispered, his mouth close to hers. "Play dead."

Shirley bucked, turning into a wildcat, and tried to fight him off. Her eyes told him he repulsed her and she wasn't up for this. She'd asked him to get him on the bed, and now he was there, she'd changed her fucking mind.

Slags weren't allowed to do that.

A red mist descended, like it had with the other tart last year, and he forgot about training her to his standards. He found himself squeezing her neck, gritting his teeth and watching her eyes bulge, the light going out of them second by second. She didn't get to call the shots. She was supposed to act dead so it he could fuck a corpse. Well, he'd fuck her afterwards all right.

He'd just have to find where she kept the condoms first.

---

With both gloves on, Vinny carried her from the shower and placed her on the bathroom floor. He dried her, then hung the towel nice on the rail, folded perfectly. Next up was taking her to the bed and arranging her. It took a while to get her in the right position and, so she didn't fall over, he propped pillows either side of her, plus some throw cushions she must use for decoration. He didn't see the point of those, but women were weird and liked them.

He spent the next couple of hours cleaning her flat. In the wardrobe, he found a pop-up washing basket, the stiff linen kind. That annoyed him. Why hadn't she used the fucking thing? He put her dirty clothes in it then prowled the rooms to make sure everything was exactly as he preferred it.

Then he sat in the living room with a cup of tea to wait out the hours.

She needed to pass through rigor mortis before he fucked her again.

He loved his women cold.

# Chapter Twenty-Eight

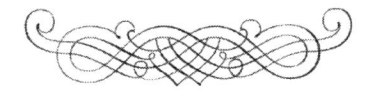

Jonathan walked into The Eagle about seven o'clock. Sonny propped up the bar.

*How does his wife put up with him never being at home and always in the boozer?*

The irony of that wasn't lost on him.

"How's it going, mate?" Sonny asked. "Been in bed? Your hair's all sticking up."

Jonathan smoothed back his hair and ducked to check his reflection in the mirror behind the bar. Appearance suitable, he said, "Yeah, I've been in bed. Gracie's been round. Now keep your bloody voice down. Jack's earwigging."

Sonny looked suitably told off and smirked. "You're a saucy bugger. So, it's love, is it?"

"I told you, I liked her right from the start. Now then, I think it's your turn to buy me a beer. I bought the last one yesterday."

"Memory like a God knows what, you've got. I thought you'd forget, because you were half-cut when you left here."

"I wasn't as pissed as you might think, so get the beers in."

After chatting and discussing the latest events, Jonathan deemed it time he was off. A taxi sailed by as he walked out of the door, and he hailed it. Getting in, he said, "Vandelies Road."

The cabbie pulled off. "I hear Rook's got a contract out on Cardigan. Dangerous."

"What?" Jonathan leant towards the open Perspex partition. Why hadn't Sonny heard about this and passed it on? "I think you've got it wrong. Cardigan's got a contract out on Rook."

The cabbie nodded sagely, and the journey continued in silence.

The taxi stopped. Jonathan climbed out and went to the window to pay his fare.

The driver waved the proffered money away. "No charge to you."

"Eh? Why not?"

"Because you gave me all the information I needed."

The taxi sped off, leaving Jonathan reeling. The cabbie was in either Rook's or Findley's pay.

*Shit.*

He cast a glance in the direction of Cardigan's house, wondering if he should tell him what had happened. Nah, best he kept out of it. He wearily went to his own home, though it didn't feel like it. Home was where he grew up. Home was where The Eagle stood at the end of the road. Home was where Gracie visited.

He put the key in the lock and stepped inside the hallway.

Leona bore down on him.

"Still awake?" he asked. "You're usually in bed by now."

"Come in here. I want some straight answers."

With his mind still spinning from the cabbie's remarks, he followed her into the sitting room, where she'd planted herself, feet apart, on the rug in front of the fireplace.

"Are you having an affair with Rebecca Lynchwood?" Her cheeks turned red.

The question caught him off guard. He burst out laughing. "Me? Having an affair with Rebecca? Don't be mental. Why would I want to saddle myself with another old bird?" The words were out before he'd had the chance to think about what he was saying.

"Old bird? Is that what you think of me? You think it's funny I'm upset?" Her face took on a scheming look—eyes narrowed, lips pursed. "If you're not careful who you keep company with, then you'd better suffer the consequences. If I so much as get a whiff of you being with another woman, I'll tell my father to retract his orders for your precious beer. From what I hear, you'd be bankrupt then."

Jonathan stopped laughing.

She smiled. "You don't find it so funny now, do you, when your business is on the line. Maybe you'll think a little more seriously before you try to put one over on me. Remember, I'm a Cardigan, and nobody messes with us." She stormed out.

Jonathan chuckled, regardless of her tirade. What he'd heard from the cabbie meant he'd sell his beer to other people once Cardigan was dead, his warning not to buy from him meaning nothing to them then. And as for Jonathan being remotely interested in Rebecca, it was a complete joke.

He went to the kitchen for a glass of water.

Seriously now, he had a think. He'd better watch himself. His happy-go-lucky attitude had been noticed by his wife, and she'd suspected an affair from that. Being that she was so paranoid about Rebecca anyway, and he'd shared Rebecca's box at the theatre, obviously Leona had put two and two together and come up with a lot more than four.

He almost felt sorry for her.

Her threats about the beer orders were just that, threats. She wouldn't risk losing him. No, Leona wouldn't do any such thing, he was sure of it.

# Chapter Twenty-Nine

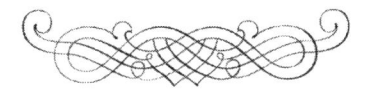

Vinny had waited ages for Shirley to go slack again. He'd contemplated doing her while she was stiff, but that wouldn't work. He probably wouldn't be able to get it up. Hours had passed since he'd killed her, and she'd be due at The Angel now, ready to please all the men except him.

He used Shirley's phone—the dopey cow didn't have a PIN—and opened the messaging app. Scrolled to Peony's name, although she had her down as Peony/Debbie. He tapped out a message, pleased with himself. If he kept this up for long enough, he could shag Shirley for a day or so—not much longer, though. She'd smell after a while like that other tart.

He stared at the message.

Shirley: *Got some kind of bug. Sorry to leave it to the last minute, but I won't be in for a while. Can one of the other girls take over my customers?*

He hit SEND.

One came back.

Peony/Debbie: *Yeah. If you need anything, let me know.*

Shirley: *I'll be all right.*

Debbie must be busy, because she didn't send another. He'd bought time before the nosy cow came snooping, maybe arriving with some bloody soup or Lucozade like his mum used to buy him as a kid when he was ill.

Vinny switched the phone off and went into the bedroom. He gave Shirley a prod or two—she was still a bit rigid. The internet had told him it could be longer than twelve hours, and while he was antsy to get going with her, this development was to his advantage. He could play with her a bit later, until the slag from the bottom flat came home. Floppy Hair kept normal hours, so he'd be asleep when Vinny left, and the woman on the top floor still hadn't come back.

He was safe as houses.

"I know I said I like you rigid, Shirl, but this is taking the piss."

He laughed and walked out of the bedroom. She had some microwave meals in the fridge. He'd have one of those to pass the time. A nice lasagne and some of those potato wedges. It beat the Super Noodles he had at his place.

Then he had to nip out, make a nuisance of himself.

Alibis were important.

# Chapter Thirty

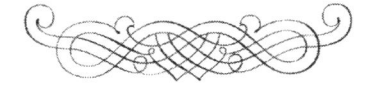

Debbie sat behind the reception desk, shifting clients about. Shirley had messaged to say she was ill, and while Debbie felt sorry for her, the late notice meant she had to scrabble to reassign the men. Luckily, it wasn't a night where a customer had specified Shirley, so there wouldn't be any sad faces with her giving them to one of the others.

Iris, blonde hair still perfect—her customer liked to do the business up against the window while he stared at the graveyard beyond, only touching her with his hands on her waist—wandered out of her room with the bloke beside her. His grey suit, white shirt, and black tie all looked as pressed as they had when he'd arrived. Iris had said he didn't even take his trousers off, just lowered the zip, and he always produced a piece of A4 from his briefcase with a hole cut out of the middle. He fed his dick through it so his trousers didn't get dirty once he disposed of the condom.

Debbie held her hand up to let Iris know she needed to speak to her, then rounded the desk, all smiles, to escort the man out of the parlour. Once he'd left, she turned to Iris. "Shirley's not in tonight, she isn't well, so you need a quicker shower than usual because you have to take Tommy Toes."

"Tommy Toes?" Iris frowned.

"Hmm. Shirley said he likes her playing This Little Piggy with his trotters. Bloody weirdo."

"Fuck. Just what I need. What time's he here?"

Debbie checked her watch. "Five minutes."

Iris sighed and walked into her room, calling out, "No rest for the wicked."

Debbie laughed and returned to her seat. She picked her phone up to reply to Shirley again but thought better of it. The poor cow might be in bed. Best not to disturb her.

Instead, she continued shifting clients around and would let Lavender and Lily know what was going on once they'd finished with their current men. It'd be a busy night for the girls, but the extra money wouldn't be sniffed at.

The CCTV monitor caught her attention, and she shuddered at Tommy Toes strutting down the corridor. She stood and went to the door, pressing the buzzer that unlocked it. Door open, she smiled at him, although inside she cringed. Just imagining him asking her girls to pinch his toes and wiggle them…no, she wouldn't think about it.

"Good evening," she said in her Peony voice.

"Evening."

She let him inside. "I'm afraid Shirley isn't in tonight."

"What's up with her?"

"She's got a bug so stayed home. Iris has agreed to take you."

"Right. I like her."

"Have a seat. She'll be with you in a moment."

He sat on one of the sofas, and Iris came out, a waft of perfume tagging along behind her. She approached Tommy, took his hand, and led him into her room.

Debbie sighed with relief that the news had gone okay with him. She was about to have a sit down when the door buzzed. She frowned—no one else was due for half an hour, and she was gagging for a cuppa. She leant over the desk and looked at the monitor.

"Fucking hell," she muttered.

Vinny was here, the last person she wanted to deal with. Hadn't he taken her threat to tell Cardigan seriously?

Clearly not.

She opened the door and glared at him. "You're barred."

He held a hand up to placate her. "Give me a second, will you? I just want to see Shirley, that's all. I miss her."

"You watch her enough down that alley, so it's not like you haven't seen her, is it."

"What?"

"Don't play dumb. She's seen you and told me."

"I don't go anywhere near no alley."

"What about bothering her at her front door then? Didn't you do that either?"

"Yeah, but that was just to ask whether I could come back."

"The answer's still no. Now fuck off. I'm definitely telling Cardigan about this. You're taking the piss. How did you even get in? I told my staff you're not welcome, even in the pub."

He looked like he wanted to cry. "Please, just let me talk to her for a second. I need to say sorry again, make it all okay."

She slammed the door on him. Where did he get off?

Shaking, despite making out she was hard as nails in front of him, she phoned Cardigan and told him everything.

"Leave it to me," he said. "I'll tell The Brothers."

She knew he wouldn't let her down. "Thanks. It's just, he's not taking no for an answer, and I'm worried about Shirley. She didn't want me to tell you."

"Like she didn't with the cutter. Silly girl shouldn't be keeping that sort of shit to herself. I don't want nutters on my manor, so how am I meant to get rid of them if she won't let me in on who they are? I've got a suspicion it wasn't Mickey who sliced her, so there are feelers out. I won't say more than that."

"Okay."

"What are you up to?" he asked.

She smiled. "The usual."

"I'll come down then, have a cuddle."

*Cuddle, my arse.* "See you in a bit then."

"You will indeed, Treacle."

# Chapter Thirty-One

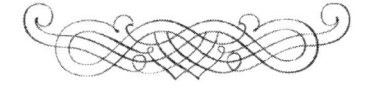

Another day had gone by without a sighting of Mickey.

"We haven't seen hide nor hair of him," George said, dogged off it was time for a visit from Cardigan and Sam yet again.

Cardigan's face took on a hardened appearance. "Well, you're not looking in the right places then, are you?"

Greg glanced incredulously at Cardigan. "There's only so many places we can check, and only so many people we can trust to ask, and with you wanting it kept quiet, what else are we supposed to do?"

Cardigan bristled at Greg's tone. "I see your point, but he's playing silly buggers. The word's out that I'm on his tail, so they've put him into hiding."

George reckoned it was time to let Cardigan know the latest bit of news. "I've heard Harry Findley's out gunning for you on behalf of Mickey. A rumour that hasn't spread far and wide yet, but you just don't know, do you."

Cardigan cracked a creepy smile. "Findley's after me? Don't make me laugh. He's like a bloody stick insect. I'd only have to breathe on him and he'd snap."

"Well, at least you know," George said, sombre. "Findley's looks can be deceiving. He can take care of himself all right."

Cardigan stood deep in thought. "If you hear any more about that side of things, let me know. And keep your ear to the ground regarding Rook.

Have you ever thought that if you find Findley, you find Rook?"

George finally got proper annoyed. "Of course we have. What d'you take us for? We're professionals. We can't find Mickey either. But it won't be long before we get those two worms out of the woodwork, and when we do, the job'll be done, you mark my words."

Cardigan nodded as if satisfied. "If you find any truth in this Findley bollocks, tell me, then I'll get you to do him an' all. I'm having none of it."

"Whatever you say," George said, weary.

Cardigan left with Sam in tow.

George turned to Greg. "He's getting right on *my* nerves now. Who does he think he is, shouting his mouth off? Stupid bastard." He lit a cigarette and inhaled deeply, pacing their living room.

"You've finally seen the light then? D'you know what? I reckon even if we do find Findley or Rook, we should keep our mouths shut. Let them do the bugger over. He's paid us well over the odds with his deposit already, more than he usually would for the whole job. We haven't lost anything."

George sucked on his smoke. "If he pisses me off once more, I might just do that."

# Chapter Thirty-Two

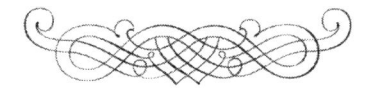

Cardigan left the house, irate. Sam remained quiet, and Cardigan climbed into the car. Pulling away from the kerb, Sam took it upon himself to drive towards the office, but Cardigan had other ideas.

"Take me to The Eagle, Sam. I feel like going back to my roots."

Sam swung the car in a U-turn and headed in the other direction.

Cardigan clenched his jaw. "Never, never have I had a job that's taken so long. I'll be a laughingstock if this lark carries on. Those twins had better get their arses in gear, or feathers'll be flying. I'll go out and personally get Rook and Fartarse myself."

Sam sighed. "If you don't mind me saying, I think you'd better leave it to The Brothers. They've never let you down before. The job'll get done, don't you worry."

Cardigan puffed out a breath. "Yeah, you're right. Ah, The Eagle. It's like coming home."

Sam parked in front of the pub, and Cardigan got out. He waited for Sam to lock up, and they both entered the boozer.

"Ron, my old son," Jack said. "How've you been?"

Cardigan felt at ease straight away, back in one of the best pubs he'd ever bought. It had taken all his wiles to get hold of it, but he'd been determined to have it. Him being brought up down this way, this had been one of his regular haunts in his heyday.

"I'm fine, Jack. How're you? Business is good, I know, but how are you yourself?"

"I'm all right, thanks. Enjoying life. Old Jonathan comes in here every night. I reckon he takes after you, because this place is his favourite."

"Well, if he's in here, he's keeping out of trouble. Who's he with?"

"Sonny Bates, as usual. They sink a few pints together and then go home."

"Good, good. Right, I want a whiskey chaser with lots of ice. I've had a bit of bother, so I need a stiff one."

Jack leant forward and lowered his voice. "I don't want to put a dampener on things, but I heard Findley's on the lookout."

Cardigan set his face in a hard grimace. The earlier report from George and Greg had now been confirmed. "I know, mate. You've just put the final nail in his coffin. The Brothers told me about it. I know what to do now, because before I came in here, I was in a bit of a muddle."

"Sorry, I didn't mean to—"

"Don't you be sorry, Jack. It's Findley who's going to be sorry."

# Chapter Thirty-Three

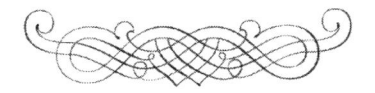

Shirley hadn't texted for two weeks with any updates, and Debbie was worried to death about her. The last time she'd got in contact, she'd said for Debbie not to come round to see her, that it was a nasty flu and she didn't want to pass it on. Well, tough, she was going round there now since radio silence had gone on for too long. She had a key for emergencies and should have used it days ago, but there was always one thing or another for her to do, and Shirley had gone down in her list of priorities. Debbie felt well guilty about it now. Shirley probably didn't have any food in the house, so the least she could do was take her a few bits.

Cardigan had sorted Vinny, who was probably in the Thames somewhere, chopped into bits, food for the fishes. She hadn't pushed for details. Just knowing Vinny was gone was all that mattered. The hunt for Mickey and Harry was still ongoing.

She picked up the Waitrose carrier back full of shopping, mainly the microwave meals Shirley loved best, and left her flat, her mind eased now she could walk down the road without Vinny popping out at her any second. She turned the corner and headed along Shirley's street, shuddering halfway as she passed the cemetery. Who had Vinny thought he was, dragging her friend down there? She was glad he'd been dealt with. The man was a creep.

At Shirley's block of flats, she inserted the key and opened the communal door. A waft of something disgusting hit her, a cross between a blocked drain and rotting beef, and she had to breathe through her mouth. Thinking she'd knock at Julie's first and ask her if she'd seen Shirley, she rapped on her door. The woman herself appeared, dishevelled and in her pyjamas.

"Just got up," Julie said.

"I can see that. What the fuck is that smell?"

"Dunno. The landlord's taking his time in dealing with it. I reckon it's coming from Shirley's myself. Blocked drain or something. I've knocked, but she's not answering."

"Have you seen her *at all* in the last fortnight?" Had she been sick so much she'd fucked up the loo and drains? Was she that poorly she couldn't even pick up a phone to ask for help?

"Nope. Not heard her either. Iris said she was ill."

"Same as she said to me. I'm going up there now to check if she's okay."

"Ask her to sort that fucking drain. I can't stand the stink any longer."

Debbie couldn't imagine living with that, and she walked up the stairs, the odour stronger the higher she climbed. It was revolting, cloying, and she swore she could taste it. Holding back a heave, she entered the flat and was almost knocked on her arse. The stench was so much worse now, hanging in the air, an invisible cloud.

"Shirley?" It came out wonky as she'd said it mid-gag. "Shirley?"

Debbie went straight to the bedroom and opened the door. If she thought the smell was bad in the hallway, it was overwhelming here. Her eyes watered, and she stared across at the bed.

Shirley knelt on it, her torso curved over, her face in the pillow. Her skin…it wasn't how skin should be. A large slice down her back exposed her spinal cord, but there was no blood. Flies buzzed around her, loads of them, and maggots swarmed in the wound, some of them falling off onto the quilt.

"Oh God…" Debbie dropped the carrier bag and staggered backwards, hitting the hallway wall. She stumbled for her phone, her first thought to tell Cardigan. She jabbed his name, unable to take her attention away from the mess on the bed while the rings trilled in her ear.

"All right, Treacle?"

"No…" She gasped, a sob taking over her, and ran to the front door. "I'm at Shirley's. She's…she's dead. Fucking dead. Someone cut her back open. There's maggots and flies. She's…it stinks and—"

"I swear to fucking God, that Mickey Rook is getting right on my wick. Phone the police. Let me know when you're back at The Angel, and I'll come and see you. Don't mention Vinny bothering her to the coppers. Last thing I need is them poking about looking for him. Tell them everything bar that. Let them deal with it."

"Okay," she whispered, moving out onto the landing and closing the front door so the smell was contained. "Okay."

"I'd say take a deep breath, but I know what that particular stench is like. Get outside into the fresh air and wait."

"I'm going now."

He cut the call, and she rushed downstairs, calling the police. She'd left the bloody shopping in the hallway. Would that matter?

As the woman on the end of the line asked her questions, Debbie's mind wouldn't focus on anything but three facts: Shirley wouldn't get to build herself up by eating the meals Debbie had bought; Debbie was a shit friend for not coming round here sooner; and Shirley probably hadn't had the flu at all.

Someone else must have been using her phone.

# Chapter Thirty-Four

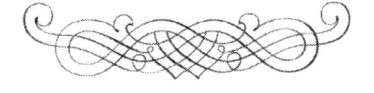

The sun shouldn't be shining, not today. Sun meant happiness, and no one standing around Shirley's grave looked happy. The police had kept her body for what seemed like ages. 'Evidence', they'd said. That was what Shirley had become in the end, nothing more than something for the authorities to pick over, trying to find clues as to who'd killed her.

While the vicar droned on, Debbie thought about what that copper had told her in confidence. Detective Allan. He'd come to see her at the parlour as a courtesy, in case some nutter was going about killing 'people like her'. He knew massages didn't happen on the premises, unless you included dicks, but he'd said that wasn't his concern. Keeping Debbie and her girls safe was.

The sex worker killed last year was his second cousin, and it had hit him hard. He just wanted to make sure no other family had to go through what his had—his cousin's and Shirley's deaths were the same, right down to their exposed spines.

The news was grim—and fucking creepy. Shirley had been washed after she'd died, and the cut to her back had occurred then, too. That was why Debbie hadn't seen any blood on the bed, but as the copper mentioned, the killer had probably washed it all away, maybe taken the sheets with him, as freshly washed ones and a new quilt were used once he'd finally finished with her.

There was evidence of sexual activity after death, too, something that had churned Debbie's stomach at the time—and still did when she thought about it. Whoever had done this had tidied and cleaned the flat, using bleach, leaving no trace of them behind, not even in the dust catcher of the hoover, or the hose, which had been washed out in Domestos. Lemon scent, apparently.

God, the things they could find out.

What Debbie hadn't understood was the pose, and she'd said as much.

"There's a suspicion it's to do with subservience," Allan had said. "The victims bowing down to them. Obviously, this information stays between you and me."

She'd nodded.

"Our profiler reckons the spine thing is the killer showing Sheila's backbone—as in, she may have resisted his efforts to make her do what he wanted, therefore, the spine on show is telling the police she died because she had a pair of balls on her. If she'd done as she was told, she'd still be alive."

"That's fucking sick." She'd paced her room in the parlour, desperate for Cardigan to come so she could tell him about this. Sod keeping it to herself. If it was Mickey who'd done it and not Vinny, he needed finding.

All in all, it was a nasty affair, and Debbie would forever live with the guilt of not suggesting Shirley came to live with her for a while until Vinny and Mickey had been dealt with. If only she'd done that. If only…

"Ashes to ashes, dust to dust…"

She stared across at Cardigan, who was on the fringes at the back. He nodded at her, and she did the same back. Maybe he was telling her they were closer to finding Mickey. The fucker had gone to ground, hiding away after what he'd done, living, breathing, when it should be Shirley doing that. If Debbie saw him before Cardigan, Sam, or The Brothers, she'd kill him herself.

She blinked. It was over, people walking away, and she joined them, silently saying sorry to Shirley, promising she'd be a better friend to the other girls to make up for her part in this. Shirley would tell her to fuck off, Debbie wasn't her keeper, and to stop blaming herself, so maybe that was what she'd do.

Cardigan waited for her behind a tree, Sam a few feet away. Allan got into his car, staring over at them, and Debbie waved at him as if to say: *It wasn't Cardigan*. Allan returned the wave then drove off.

"Any news?" Debbie whispered.

Cardigan sighed. "Not a fucking dicky bird on where Mickey is, but I made sure word got out that I'm after him and Harry. I'm going to do them for this—whether it was really Vinny or not. The money doesn't matter now, Shirley does. That poor cow didn't deserve this."

"No, she didn't."

"I've got a problem, though." He grimaced. "There's a hit out on me."

"What?" Her heart tripled its speed. "Who?"

He laughed. "He won't get anywhere near me, not with Sam around. But listen, in case shit goes down and I don't come out of this—"

"Don't say that, I—"

"I do bad things, Treacle, and expect this in my line of work. So I've got things in motion. The Angel's yours now, got it?"

It took a second or two for that to sink in. "Wh…?"

"Someone'll drop the papers round for you to sign. Did you know you bought it off me for a pound?" He laughed again, quietly. "You've been good to me and deserve the best."

Tears misted her eyes. Cardigan appeared as a hazy grey blob. "Nothing will happen to you." She had to tell herself that. She'd got too damn attached to him, and the thought of something happening wasn't allowed. "You'll find whoever it is first."

"That's the plan. Now, bugger off home. There's been enough tears for one day."

She smiled as he walked away to his car, and she went to where Lily, Lavender, and Iris waited. They walked to The Angel where the wake was being held. Shirley didn't have any family except them, and Debbie was buggered if her mate would go to the next world without a good send-off. The parlour would be closed tonight, and they'd drink the evening away instead, taxis for her girls later in case Mickey had a mind to kill them, too—that was what everyone thought, that he'd murdered Shirley, but she was conflicted, what with Vinny acting weird.

Fuck. Debbie couldn't live on her nerves like this for much longer.

# Chapter Thirty-Five

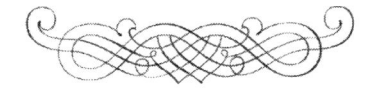

Leona picked the mail up from the mat and dropped the letters on the kitchen table. She opened a cream envelope first and pulled out a plain piece of white paper, large and folded in half. She stared at the page, her heart hammering too fast and tears stinging her wide eyes. Instead of being written or typed, the words were made of newspaper clippings, carefully cut out and pasted on.

> YOU NEED TO WATCH YOURSELF, LEONA
> WHAT GOES AROUND COMES AROUND

Stomach lurching, she dropped the note and gripped the table edge. Her head spun, and the words merged. Sick to her stomach, she took in deep breaths.

Who on earth would want to send her *that*? And what did the cryptic message mean? She frantically tried to sort out the thoughts racing through her head, her hand held to her chest and her mouth hanging open.

A knock sounded at the front door, pushing her heart to beat faster.

*Should I answer it? What if it's the letter sender?*

Leona shoved her chair back, rose on wobbly legs, and walked cautiously into the hallway. The silhouette of a large frame stood on her doorstep.

"Open up, I know you're in there."

She let out her breath in relief. Her father. Composing herself, she opened the door. He walked in carrying some letters.

"There's a bit of mail here for you. It came to mine last week, but I didn't get the chance to pop them over. I've been a bit busy." He handed her the slim bundle.

Leona's stomach contracted again. Amongst the pile was another cream envelope, her name and address typed on the front.

"What's up with you? You look a bit off colour. Aren't pregnant, are you?" He laughed.

Leona swallowed excess spittle. "No, I am not pregnant. Jonathan and I *do not* have that sort of relationship, thank you very much." She stalked into the kitchen and snatched up the letter she'd left there. She didn't want him to see it. He'd find out who it was and… No, she'd go through the proper channels with this, if that was what she decided. She needed to think about it.

She shoved the letter into the nearest drawer and turned round. Her father filled the kitchen doorway.

"What's up with you, eh?" he growled. "Make your old man a cup of tea. I'm bloody gasping."

The chore took her mind off her problem a little, but she itched to open the cream envelope he'd brought, at the same time loath to in case it contained worse than the first. Pouring out tea, the pot still hot from when she'd filled it for her breakfast, she passed the cup to her father, who'd plonked himself wearily on one of the kitchen chairs.

She casually sorted through the mail. The postmark on this new letter indicated it was the first one she was supposed to have received. Maybe they'd tell a story. Perhaps the one she'd already opened would make sense once she read the first. She put it on the side.

Her father drummed his fingertips on the tabletop.

Annoyed at the sound, she said, "Was there any particular reason for your visit other than dropping off my post?"

He stared at her in surprise. "Well, I did want to discuss something with you, but if you're not in the mood, I'll drink my tea and bugger off. I know when I'm not wanted."

"No, no, it's all right." She felt the complete opposite. "I'll have to be going out soon, though. I have various hospital visits to do today."

"What I've got to say won't take more than two minutes." His face took on a grave look. "I've got my insurance details all up to date, and my will's in the safe, same combination number as I've always had."

"What on earth are you telling me that for?"

"Someone's after me."

Leona readied herself to launch into one of her tirades.

He lifted a hand to stop her. "Don't go on. I know my lifestyle isn't what you'd like, but there you have it. I wanted you to know I've left mostly everything to you: this house, my house, and all the pubs except one. I don't want The Eagle going to strangers, so bear that in mind if you sell. The Angel now belongs to someone else."

He rose to take his leave.

"Who?" she asked.

"None of your business."

*It'll be that bloody Debbie.*

Worried by this turn of events, she ignored The Angel thing. "What do you mean, someone's after you? What have you been up to?"

"Don't go fretting yourself. Has anyone ever got the better of me?"

"No."

"Well, then, don't worry about it. I needed to make sure you knew what I wanted, just in case."

Leona looked at him. She hadn't realised how much she'd relied on him since her mother's death. Even though she most certainly didn't agree with his lifestyle, he was there to protect her if things went wrong.

"Have you got everything under control?" she asked.

"Just about. One or two minor details, and the one who's after me'll be sorted himself. Keep your chin up and get off to the hospital."

He walked from the kitchen and made his way to the front door. Leona followed.

He turned to her. "I'm not one to make a fuss, never have been, but I never told your mother what I should have, and it was too late. I love you, and don't you forget it."

Tears sprang to her eyes, and she dashed them away. Unable to make such a show of affection herself, she said briskly, "Good."

She closed the door on him and rushed to the kitchen, more pressing things on her mind. Snatching up the cream envelope, she ripped it open. Her breath caught in her throat.

I KNOW SOMETHING YOU DON'T KNOW

# Chapter Thirty-Six

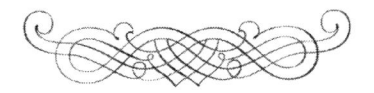

Harry and Mickey were keeping their heads down at a safe house. Word had spread and reached their ears. Cardigan was out for their blood. At first, Harry had taken the news that came through their contact, Bill Haynes, a cabbie, with a pinch of salt. But when Harry had been assured that the word had come from Cardigan's son-in-law, he reckoned the outlook was bleak to say the least. He'd wanted to get Cardigan long ago, but Mickey had stalled him, saying it'd look too much like their doing should the police get involved. A revenge attack didn't go down too well with the local filth.

With time on their hands, they idled the hours away until Harry sent out the message that he wanted to meet Cardigan. He'd had the weapon delivered—a gun that'd hit his target spot-on. He'd planned for every eventuality, and all his options had been schemed and worked out. They had enough time to do it.

The question was, when?

The letterbox clattered, indicating the arrival of two local papers. Confined as they were, in this out-of-the-way place with no internet, they'd originally fought over who'd read it first. Harry then had the foresight to order two, especially after the last fiasco, which had nearly come to blows.

Getting up to retrieve the papers, Harry slouched into the hallway and picked them up off the mat. He walked into the sitting room and casually tossed one at Mickey.

Harry sat in an armchair to read his from cover to cover. If boredom reigned supreme he'd read it again, just to make sure he hadn't missed anything.

The headlines screamed at him from the page. There'd been a murder, and a cold-blooded one at that. Reading the details, Harry was shocked. "Fucking hell. Some tart's been offed."

He continued to read, as Mickey, too, was engrossed in the saga splashed across the front page.

Harry then blurted out, "Jesus Christ. It's only Shirley. I can't bleedin' believe it. A while ago, it was. Why are they only reporting it now?" He shook his head and chanced a peek at Mickey.

He'd gone white and didn't look well.

"What the hell's wrong with you?" Harry said.

"It isn't my bloody day. You know what's going to happen now, don't you? Those bloody brothers will think it was my doing. I said I'd see her sorted."

"Fucking hell, Mickey. What did you have to go and say a thing like that for?"

"I didn't bloody well mean it. I'd have done it ages ago if I really meant it."

"Not necessarily, you wanker. Look how long it took the twins to sort you out. And that was because you threatened her an' all. What a mess we're in. I'll just have to kill Cardigan quicker than I intended, that's all. Shit."

"And The Brothers? What about them? They'll still be searching for me, even when Cardigan's dead and buried."

"You should think of these things when you tell a Brother you're going to get a woman done over. You know they don't hold with that sort of thing. It's a good job I'm your mate. Most blokes wouldn't save your arse after this. Poor Shirley. I've been with her myself. Tasty in the sack. What a waste."

"You slimy git." Mickey crumpled the paper on his lap. "You didn't tell me you'd slept with one of my girlfriends."

"I didn't think I'd have to. She's a bloody prosser, that's what they're there for." Harry frowned. "*Was* a prosser."

They sat in silence while reading the rest of the article.

Then Mickey said, "Whoever it was sliced her back up an' all. Filthy bastard."

"She isn't going to need it where she's gone," Harry said quietly.

"I know, but it isn't the point."

"Shall we put the feelers out and find out who did it?" Harry asked.

"Yeah. We'll do it for old time's sake."

# Chapter Thirty-Seven

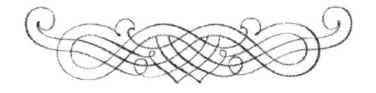

"That bloody Mickey's got a lot to answer for," George barked.

Cardigan had come to visit George and Greg, as per usual, and they were discussing Shirley's murder.

"But we don't even know if it was him who did it," Greg said.

"You heard him," George sniped. "He said he was going to get her once and for all. He just bided his bloody time so we'd think it wasn't him."

"Hold up, hold up. You reckon that slimy ponce, Mickey Rook, had Shirley bloody Richmond offed?" Cardigan asked.

He stared around menacingly at the group. George scowled, and Greg seemed ashamed, as if what George had said was ludicrous. Sam had his usual noncommittal look about him.

No one answered.

Cardigan huffed. "What's this about hearing what he said? Has something been going on that I don't know about?"

Greg sighed. "As you now, Rook was seeing Shirley once upon a time. They argued about something or other, and that was the end of it. Rook threatened to beat her up, told us about it, then lo and behold, her face gets cut."

"Get it right, Greg," George butted in. "Rook said: 'However long it takes, I'm going to get that slag.'" He balled his hands. "I told you, he's just been waiting. Took him long enough, but it's done now."

"Give me the sodding paper and let me have a read." Cardigan was getting angrier with regards to Rook. He was initially under the impression

Vinny had killed her so had ignored all the rumours about Mickey. Now, more than ever, he wanted to kill the little bastard.

"It could be a one-off attack by a punter," Greg said.

Cardigan couldn't have them linking this to Vinny. They'd look for him and find out he was missing. It might reach a pig's ears.

"One-off, my arse," George said. "Listen to the facts. One: Rook says he's going to get Shirley Richmond one day. Two: Rook's holed up somewhere without the availability of women so he's bleedin' desperate, going to see her for a shag. Three: Shirley would've let him go with her, regardless of what he said, if he was paying. Four: She's been sliced down her spine, which is about all Rook could manage, little ponce that he is. Five: I bet her money's been nicked. Rook hasn't been able to work. I reckon it's down to him, no bones about it."

Cardigan nodded, chuffed George had said what he'd wanted to. "I'm as convinced as you. We'll have to step up our efforts to flush him out of hiding. Maybe now you'll get your arse in gear, George, and finally find the wanker. It's been too long."

George took exception. "Are you saying we haven't been doing our job properly? We haven't seen him since we did him the last time."

Cardigan held back his temper. "Don't get aerated. Just make sure you find him now. I want that villain dead. Oh, and there's a change of plan. Get the Shirley Richmond confession out of him before you chop his knackers off. That should be sufficient torture in itself. I'm off. Let me know if you hear anything."

---

Cardigan stormed out, leaving George and Greg standing feet apart, glaring out of the window, waiting for the door to close and watching until the car drove away.

"I don't reckon it was Rook, George. It's not his style."

George sighed. He could see it clearly; Greg couldn't. "Well, you wouldn't, would you. You want to see the best in everyone at the moment. Bar Cardigan, who seems to be the only one that gets your goat. It was Rook, and I'll prove it when we get our hands on him. That's if you're still in business with me?"

"Course I am, but I don't like going round chopping off innocent men's nuts, just because my brother thinks they've killed a prosser. Wait until we see another report in the paper before we root him out for that. Or better still, go and see that bent copper friend of yours. He'll be able to give you the lowdown on what's what."

"I don't need to go and see Rod Clarke. He won't know anything."

"You just don't want to see Clarke in case he tells you something you don't want to hear. You need to go and get your head tested, mate. Like I've said before, there's something seriously wrong with you lately."

George let the remark slide. If anyone else had said that, he'd kill them on the spot, but his brother was just mentioning something that'd been bothering George lately, too. He reckoned he was losing his mind. He'd been dreaming up a lot of sordid and nasty things to do to people for when Cardigan asked him to sort someone out. If Cardigan wanted a kneecapping done, he'd go one step further and break his leg as well. If Cardigan wanted all the fingers broken, he'd have to break the whole hand and the wrist. Cardigan didn't seem to mind—he was getting a few freebies thrown in. Greg didn't have anything to do with the extras, and more often of late, George had been thinking he was going insane from all the carnage he engaged in each day. His mind was turning, and he knew it. But there didn't seem to be anything he could do to stop it.

Looking at his brother now, the only person he'd ever admit this to, he said, "I know I need to see a shrink, but not just yet. There're demons in me that won't go away. I'll get it sorted, but I want that little shit Rook first. Just let me do that, and I'll get my head tested."

Greg stared. "I'll be with you all the way."

"I know you will. Right. We need to put the frighteners on some of Rook's mates. It's the only way we're going to get anywhere."

"So, when do we start?"

"Now."

# Chapter Thirty-Eight

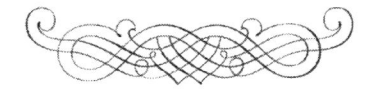

"Give him the note personally, and make sure he reads it in front of you. I want an immediate response. No poncing around," Harry belted out to Sid Dempsey, one of his runarounds.

Sid was an unassuming-looking man, thinning brown hair that was just getting its first streaks of grey. Brushed back from his face, it showed how he was receding, and his ferret-type features had Harry thinking of a slinky, sly animal. Wheeling and dealing for most of his working life, Sid stole the majority of goods that Harry and Mickey sold. He earned commission from providing the nicked stuff, and now they weren't working as such, Sid needed the cash he'd earn from running this message.

"Right, so I hand him the note and wait for a reply? That right?" Sid asked, dumb as fuck.

Harry nodded. "That's it. Now go to his office. He'll only have Sam with him, and if you get any trouble, let me know, however small it may seem to you. It'll go on the long list I've got of all the naughty things Cardigan's been doing to us over the years."

"Shall I go now?"

"Yeah."

---

"What's that freaky fairy doing here?" Cardigan asked.

Sam went over to the office window and peered out. "He's on his own." He paused. "And he's come from that Findley. He's in his car."

"I can fucking see that," Cardigan grated out. "Yeah."

"I wonder what the slimebag wants?"

Sam gestured in the direction of the front of the office. "You'll find out in a minute. He's just about to knock."

Sid's knuckles rapped against the frosted glass.

"Who is it?" Cardigan barked.

"Sid Dempsey," came the muffled reply.

"What d'you want?"

"I've got a message from Findley."

"But you haven't got an appointment." Cardigan smirked at Sam.

"I think you'll want to read the note, though," Sid said, his voice whiny. "Findley said I wasn't to leave without a reply."

Cardigan held in his laughter, and his body shook. "Oh, he did, did he? Well then, you'd better come in and tell me more." He nodded to Sam, giving permission for the door to be opened.

Sid walked in, his small face averted.

Cardigan stared at him. "You take the piss out of me today, and you'll know all about it."

Sid froze.

Cardigan wanted to punch the little bastard. "Give me the note then, you fucking great prat."

Sid handed it over, his hand shaking.

Cardigan placed the note on his desk, unopened. "Want a drink? Tea, coffee, or something stronger?"

Sid swallowed. "I'll have a cuppa, thanks. Two sugars." He cleared his throat and added, "Please."

*I should think so.* "Sam, make our good friend here a drink, will you? He looks parched. Got a dry mouth, have you?"

Sid tried to swallow again, but it appeared there was no saliva. "Yeah, I have as it happens."

The kettle had not long boiled, so it didn't take long for Sam to make the brew. They waited in uncomfortable silence—uncomfortable for Sid anyway—then Sam passed him a cup. Taking it, Sid sipped and looked over the rim at Cardigan, who eyed him with a smile.

"Did you poison this?" Sid asked.

"Fuck did I," Sam said. "You watched me make it, divvo."

Cardigan bit back a chuckle. "So, Sid, did you have to meet up with Findley or do you know where he is?"

Sid took a deep breath. "I knew where to go from a contact. But I can't reveal where they are. You know how it is."

*Oh, I know how it is all right.*

Cardigan glanced sideways at his right-hand man. "Oh, Sam. I forgot. You've got to do that phone call for me. Go outside, because me and Sid here are having a private conversation. We don't want to hear you in the background, do we, Sid?"

Sid shook his head, and Sam left the office, locking the door behind him.

"Now, getting back to our conversation. Yeah, I do know how it is. Your loyalty is a good sign. I admire you for it." He didn't.

He chuckled inwardly. Sid looked as though he wondered whether Cardigan was being sincere, trying to gauge what he was up to. Sid had very nearly gulped all his tea down, surely burning his mouth in the process.

Cardigan decided he'd frightened the poor ferret enough. He leant forward and picked up the envelope. "I'd better be reading this then. You can get on with whatever you've got to do. I can't promise a reply, though. It depends on what's inside this envelope."

"But—" Sid worked his mouth, panic showing on his face.

"No buts about it. If I don't want to reply, are you going to make me?"

"No, I'm bloody not," he blurted.

The key slid in the lock, and Sam came back in, nodding at Cardigan. He went and stood in his usual place to the right, behind his boss.

Cardigan sniffed. "I'll see you all right, Sid. If I don't reply to this note, you can give Findley a message from me. How's that? Then you'll not go back with nothing to say. You can tell him I was going to beat the crap out of you because you made such a fuss about it. Then you'll still look good to him, won't you."

"I don't get paid without a reply," Sid said, dejected.

Cardigan shook his head. "I'll give you some money. What are you doing working for the likes of him? Don't get paid without a reply? Findley's not a very good boss, is he."

"Well…" Sid shifted from foot to foot. "I took the job on as it was offered. If I don't do it as the man said, I don't get paid. Simple as that."

"I'd best be opening the envelope then, hadn't I?" Cardigan slit it with his small knife and took out a piece of paper. He read it and roared with laughter. "I'll put you out of your misery. I'll write a reply."

He whipped out a notepad from his desk drawer, and, holding the pad up so Sid couldn't see, he jotted down a few words. He placed it in an envelope and put Findley's name on it.

Taking it, Sid made to leave. "Thanks. I'll be off then."

"Nice doing business with you. Sam, give the gentleman a hundred quid then see him out."

---

The Brothers had their van engine going in readiness for Sid Dempsey's departure from Cardigan's office.

Hands on the steering wheel, George said, "He's on the move. Get going."

Greg put the van in gear and sped off to catch up with Sid who was in Findley's car—a fucking novice mistake. Keeping at a slight distance, they followed him to where Sid slowed and parked in a side road outside a small house.

"What's he doing? Why isn't he getting out?" George said.

"Perhaps he's rolling a fag or something. I don't bleedin' know." Greg scrubbed at his chin.

George leant forward. "He's getting out."

They sat in silence, George anticipating Sid entering the house he'd stopped outside. Sid left the car and walked a few paces down the street.

Greg slapped the dashboard. "The little sod's put it in the bloody postbox. Fuck me, Cardigan isn't going to be pleased. Findley's more cunning than he's been given credit for."

Sid got back into Findley's car, and George drove off, following him down the backstreets. Sid parked in a space provided for the customers outside The Grapes. He entered the pub.

Van engine off, George settled down for the wait for Sid to come back out. "Go and look through the window and see who that sod's talking to. Findley or Rook might be in there."

Greg sighed and made his way towards the pub window. He peered through one of the squares of glass then walked back, shaking his head.

Getting in, he said, "He's on his own. We've got a long wait."

George smacked the steering wheel, pain going up his arm. "Cardigan said however late it was, we're to contact him with any news. I'm prepared to wait. We're so close to finding that shit Rook, I can almost taste it."

Greg made himself comfortable. "Well, I don't know about you, but I'm having a kip."

"Do what you bloody like. I'll keep watch all night if I have to."

Sid was following his instructions to the letter. After driving the short distance from Cardigan's office to the postbox, he'd parked and got out his pen, putting Findley's hideout address under Cardigan's scrawl. He'd licked a stamp and popped the letter in the postbox, let out a sigh of relief, and went to The Grapes.

He waited at the bar.

An unobtrusive-looking bloke approached him. "Name?"

"Sid Dempsey."

"Done it?"

"Yeah."

The fella held out an envelope. Sid took it and ripped it open. The amount in there had him verging on a faint. Fucking hell. Findley must mean business to be paying him that much. Sid reflected on this little job. It'd been worth shitting himself in Cardigan's office, getting a hundred quid there, too. He wouldn't have to work for a month.

He caught the attention of a barmaid, ordered a pint of bitter, and glanced over at the man who'd given him his wages. He was on the phone. He looked round at Sid and gave him the thumbs-up. Sid received his pint with proper gratitude, offering the barmaid one for herself out of the tenner he gave her.

"I'll have a gin and tonic, thanks, darlin'," she said.

"You can have what you bloody like." Sid beamed. "I'm flush."

---

Harry received the call then slid his phone in his pocket. "We'll get the letter tomorrow, Mickey. Things are on the move."

"Don't count your chickens. You don't know what the reply says yet." Mickey sounded unsure.

"He'll do it. He won't be able to resist," Harry said, all smug.

"Let's hope he bloody does, or we're fucked."

# Chapter Thirty-Nine

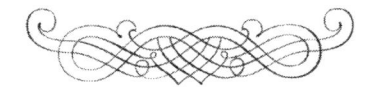

Gracie and Jonathan had eaten lunch at The Jack of Hearts. Gracie had taken the day off. The weather was hot, and they left the pub to go to their special field.

The cows had got used to them now.

*Thank fuck.*

Tartan blanket on the grass, they spread themselves out on it.

While Gracie sunbathed, he thought about the recent events. The customers he'd hoped would come to buy his beer, from as far afield as twenty miles away, hadn't materialised, leaving Cardigan as the sole buyer of his stock.

*There must be something else I can do to get away from Leona.*

He came up with blank after blank. Cardigan would have more than his guts for garters should he tell him he could no longer stand being married to his daughter. It might sound better coming from Leona herself, but she seemed content with the way things were.

She'd been in a weird mood lately, always jumpy and asking him where he was going and what time he'd be in. She'd never been that bothered before, and he was jumpy himself, wondering if she suspected, yet again, he was seeing another woman. It wouldn't be from his behaviour this time. He acted weary when around her so she'd think he was unhappy.

Gracie snapped him out of his reverie. "I'm pregnant."

Stunned—this was the last thing he fucking needed—he said, "What?"

"I'm pregnant."

Mixed emotions surged through him. He'd have to put his plans into action faster than he'd thought. What the hell was he supposed to do now? Tell her all about Leona and hope for the best? Or go through the charade of being a bigamist and marry her? No, someone would find out, and the lid would be blown off the shitty can of worms his life had become.

"What are we going to do?" he asked carefully.

"What do you want to do? I could go and get rid of it."

"Get rid of it? No. You can't do that."

"I can if it's too soon for you to want his sort of thing. I'm wondering if I want it myself."

"What d'you mean?" he asked.

"Just what I said. I'm not sure if I can cope with the idea of being a mother just yet." She sighed.

A short and awkward silence followed.

Then Jonathan said, "How long have you known?"

"I found out yesterday afternoon."

"Shall we think about it for a week or two and then decide?"

She looked down at her hands.

"Shall we go home?" Jonathan suggested.

"Yours or mine?"

"Whatever you reckon's best."

"We'll go to yours. I can't face Mum at the moment." She got up.

Jonathan followed suit and watched her fold the blanket. "She doesn't know then?"

"No," came the bland reply.

*Fuck me, can my life get any worse?*

# Chapter Forty

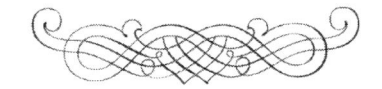

Leona had been on edge for days. She walked down the hallway to get the post from the mat, her guts going over. Another letter. The fear at what it contained was always the same. Clutching at the bundle, she went to her kitchen table.

She slowly took out the usual folded white paper, hardened and uneven from dried glue. Laid it out and read the four words, sick to her stomach. The message seemed more sinister and menacing than the other two.

JUSTICE WILL BE DONE

# Chapter Forty-One

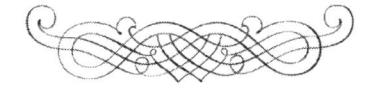

Cardigan stared at The Brothers. "Right, you all know what to do, and if there are any cockups, it's my head on the bleedin' line if they're planning to do me over. So, it's in your best interests to look after me, isn't it, because if I'm gone, you don't get as much wages unless you find someone else like me who wants you on their payroll."

He was trying to lighten the gloomy atmosphere by saying it all jovial, and if he were honest, he was feeling more than uneasy about today's meeting with Findley. It'd been made clear that Rook wouldn't be attending and Findley just wanted to hand over the poker money and be on his way. But Cardigan knew otherwise. Findley would try to do him over, while worrying where Cardigan's men were in their efforts to do *him* over first.

"We know what to do, don't you worry," Sam said.

"George, Greg, all set?" Cardigan asked.

"Yes, Ron," the twins said together, creepy as eff.

He nodded. "Right then, let's go."

---

Debbie had a ball of emotion in the pit of her stomach. It was the Christmas-morning feeling but not, more intense and nothing to do with being excited. Dread? She wasn't sure, but with Cardigan letting her know they were closer to getting Mickey and Findley, she put it down to that.

She'd signed the papers, and The Angel belonged to her. Surreal that she could now claim all the profits—from the boozer and the parlour—instead of taking a wage from Cardigan. The Angel was always packed to the gills, didn't matter which night of the week it was, and she'd soon learnt that the grand a week she used to get had gone up significantly.

Debbie had passed on some of her good fortune by lowering the room rents for the girls by one hundred quid a month, something Shirley would've approved of. She'd also upped Lisa's wages, giving her another five hundred a month. Everyone was happy.

Except Debbie. If this feeling didn't pass soon, she'd go off on one.

She phoned Cardigan. There was something she had to say before he embarked on what he'd said he'd do regarding the hit out on him. If something happened to him and she hadn't told him how she felt, she'd have another load of guilt piled on her shoulders.

"All right, Treacle. Bit busy at the minute, if you catch my drift."

"It's today?"

"Yep."

So that's what the dread was all about. "Okay, I just wanted to tell you I love you."

He laughed. "Don't you think I know that?"

*He does?* "Oh."

His chuckle sounded kind, not derisive. "I need to go. See you soon."

The line went dead.

She just had to sit tight and hope the same didn't happen to Cardigan, too.

---

"Are you sure you've got everything sorted?" Mickey asked, "because I reckon Cardigan'll know what you're up to. He'll think of everything." He was well uneasy.

Harry smiled wryly. "He's got dosh on the brain. He won't even think I won't turn up and be sighting him from over the bloody road. The minute he turns up, I'll have the bastard."

"Are you sure the gun'll work properly?" Mickey felt helpless. He'd be stuck at their hideout, unable to see or hear what was going on. Unable to do a damn thing to help.

Harry straightened his shoulders. "I told you, I've tried it out in the garden with tin cans. It goes like a ruddy dream. He'll be a goner. One pop, and he's mine." He paused and narrowed his eyes. "I hate him, d'you know that?"

Mickey nodded. "You've told me often enough. Just go and do it and come straight back here after. I'm the one stuck in here while you're doing the job, and it'll be a long wait, I can tell you." He stuck his bottom lip out.

"Just sit tight. I'll be back before you know it."

Mickey leant forward in his chair and held out his hand. Harry shook it, and Mickey clasped his free hand over their other two and squeezed. This may be the last time he saw his friend, and, after all, Harry was doing this for him. He was sticking up for him like no one ever had.

"Good luck, mate," Mickey said, getting a bit choked up.

Harry ruffled Mickey's hair and grinned. "Thanks, pal, but I assure you, I won't need it."

---

Harry was using a room in a ground-floor flat, loaned to him by a mate he could trust. He'd chosen it because of the ease he'd have in escaping once he'd fired the gun. His car was parked to the rear, the door unlocked, and he had the keys ready in his pocket for a quick getaway.

His plan was perfect. Nothing could possibly go wrong. The scene was set, and Cardigan would be arriving over the road any minute.

Scenarios went through Harry's mind. Sam would stop the car and, as instructed, Cardigan had been told to get out alone. He'd suspect something was up once Harry didn't show, and he wouldn't put it past him to wear a bulletproof vest.

But there were other fatal places to shoot.

On the other hand, Cardigan might not get out, even though this had been expressly asked for, but Harry had that covered as well. He'd just shoot the big git through the car window, and if that didn't work, he'd pull the trigger and send a bullet over there. Sam would unfortunately cop it, too. It didn't matter to Harry, and as long as Cardigan got killed, he'd have obtained his objective.

The Brothers were bound to be close by, so the exit from the back of the tower block would be ideal. The twins would be busy running across the road to where the shot had been fired and waste valuable time searching the various flats to look for the shooter.

*Twats, the pair of them.*

His palms grew sweaty. His shot would meet its mark, he was certain of that. Even if he got caught, which he reckoned was highly unlikely, it wouldn't matter. Cardigan would be dead, and everyone who ran scared of him could rest easy. Harry chuckled at the thought of people within The Cardigan Estate letting out their collective breaths.

The time had come to stop laughing. Cardigan's car drew up opposite the tower block, on the other side of the road from Harry's position. Beyond that, a field. He checked the business end of the gun wouldn't be clocked poking through the gap in the window.

His heart beat faster. Cardigan did as he'd requested and got out of the car. Alone, only the top half of him visible—he'd shielded himself behind his vehicle, the wanker. Sam sat in the driver's seat, the engine still running.

Harry aimed at Cardigan's forehead. Dead centre. Cardigan stood amazingly still, as if he really thought Harry might be turning up. He slowly pulled the trigger back, the target and aim in perfect line with one another.

Cardigan bent down to Sam's open window to talk to him.

"Shit!" Harry let out his breath and positioned himself again, straining to hear what the big man was saying.

"I'll give him one more minute, and if the little turd hasn't turned up by then, I'm going. And then I'll find him and kill him my bloody self."

Cardigan stood tall and stared straight over at Harry. The beefy fucker went to open his mouth to speak to Sam, but Harry pulled the trigger right back.

"Who're you calling a little turd?" Harry spat.

Cardigan went down, and if he wasn't dead, he soon would be. He'd hit him in the middle of his forehead. Supreme shot.

Sam got out of the car, stooped, and disappeared behind it.

Harry made his way calmly out of the flat, shoving his gun into its holdall. He walked towards his car.

Sam's shout reached him.

"George, Greg, Cardigan's down. Where the hell are you? He's killed him."

In his car, Harry smirked. He turned the engine over and muttered, "I don't give a shit where the twins are. I'm home and bloody dry." He eased away and drove in the direction of the hideout.

"I think you will give a shit where we are when you realise we're sitting in the back of your fucking car," George said, close, too close.

Harry jumped, his hands flying off the steering wheel. The car veered, and as he righted it, he said, "Shit! What the bloody hell are you two doing in here?"

"Never you mind. Now drive," Greg ordered.

"Where am I bloody going?" Harry said, his voice calm but his insides in turmoil.

"We're going for a little ride, and then we'll have a bit of a chat." George sounded at his most menacing.

Cold metal touched Harry's neck, and he almost shit himself. He glanced in the rearview mirror. Greg's revolver looked small in the hardman's hand.

"Shut up now," Greg said, "and keep going. Turn right down there, and then the next two lefts."

Harry's heart thudded in overdrive, and blood pulsed through his neck vein. He took the instructed turnings, knowing he'd find himself at his and Mickey's garage.

"Park the car in front of the garage, switch off the engine, and give the keys to me," George barked.

Harry lost no time in complying—the gun pressed harder.

"Right, what've you been playing at?" George asked. "We gather you've been a naughty boy."

"I killed Cardigan," Harry blurted, then with courage said, "And I don't care what you do to me. I've rid the place of a scumbag. If you think about it, I've done you two a bloody favour. Anyway, if you cared about your boss, you'd have gone to Sam when he called you." He turned to look at his captors.

Greg took the gun away, and Harry rubbed his neck. Greg glanced at George, who seemed to be considering what Harry had said.

George sniffed. "I think I'll pretend I didn't hear the cheek in your voice. For the life of me I don't know why, but I agree with you. What d'you you think, Greg?"

"You know what I think of Cardigan."

"Get out of the bloody car, Fartarse," George said mildly.

All three exited Harry's small runabout. With the thaw in George's manner, Harry had no urgency to escape the twins but resolved to see it through should they attack him. He'd done what he'd promised Mickey he'd do, and his only worry was that Mickey would fear the worst if he didn't get back to the hideout soon.

The Brothers stood side by side facing him, and, miraculously, George held out his hand. Wary, Harry held his out, ready to shake George's but on his guard in case George yanked his arm out of its socket. He just pumped his hand up and down and then slapped him jovially on his back.

George laughed, Greg joining him.

"What's so bleedin' funny?" Harry asked. "Come on, what the bloody hell are we laughing at?"

Greg sobered. "We're laughing because...we'd planned to kill Cardigan ourselves, but once we saw your car parked out the back of the flats... Cardigan was convinced you'd show with the money and sent us off to hide, ready to ambush you when you thought you were safe."

George smiled wide. "That's a classic, that is. We go to kill Cardigan, and you do the job for us. How did you do it, because he was wearing a vest?"

"I thought he would be, so I shot him in the head." Harry puffed out his chest.

George and Greg looked at one another.

Greg said, "He got what he deserved. He's had it coming for years. Good fucking riddance, that's all I can say. We can take over now."

George seemed happier than he had in years and handed over the car keys. "Here, you couldn't give us a lift home, could you? I don't fancy walking."

"Yeah, all right," Harry said.

They got back in the car.

Something was off. Harry said, "Tell me, what was all the gun and attitude about with me if you wanted to do him over yourself?"

Greg smiled. "George was pissed off you'd beat us to it, that's all, but at the end of the day, the main objective was Cardigan getting done."

"On second thoughts," George said as Harry drove along, "take us to the flats where we left our van."

Harry turned the car round, cursing himself for not seeing it there earlier.

George stared out of the window. "If Cardigan's anything like I think he is, he'd have given Sam instructions to call the dodgy doctor if he'd suspected he was going to be hit. He wouldn't want his mate to get any gyp from this sort of thing. The doctor'll sort it all out. The coppers won't even be looking for a murderer. You're safe, mate." He patted Findley's shoulder. "But Sam might be out on the rampage after all this lot's cleared up. Just watch out, that's my advice."

"Sam? Out on the rampage? Don't make me laugh," Greg said.

"Maybe he'll sod off altogether, then Findley here can go about his business without any worries."

"That'd be nice." Harry pulled the car up next to the twins' van and glanced about. No one around here would grass him up should there be a report of gunfire. They all knew to keep quiet.

"Thanks for the lift," Greg said.

"That's all right."

Harry watched The Brothers get into their battered old van and drive away. Not being able to resist, he left his car and walked round the side of the tower block, fully expecting to see police cars and an ambulance with lights flashing on the other side of the road. No flashing lights. No emergency service vehicles. Cardigan's car was gone. George had been right. Sam would have taken Cardigan to a bent doctor.

Harry squinted. All he saw as proof someone had been shot to death was the blood that had dripped over the kerb and onto the pavement. Sam hadn't sorted out the mess yet then.

"Slacker." Harry made his way back to his car, ready for the drive to the safe house.

The only thing that bothered him was why The Brothers hadn't asked about Mickey. Maybe with Cardigan dead, they wouldn't be after him now.

Harry could only hope.

# Chapter Forty-Two

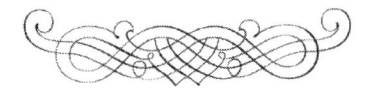

Hearing the gunshot and seeing Cardigan fall would haunt Sam for the rest of his days. Cardigan had slumped down on the pavement, and Sam wedged himself out and bent down to his boss and friend.

Cardigan had landed on his side. A pool of crimson seeped along the tarmac. Sam had shaken him then rolled him onto his back. His staring, lifeless eyes looked vacantly at him, and the hole in his forehead had dribbled blood. The back of his head was missing, some brains and whatnot on the grass beside the path.

Sam had shouted for the twins, and, getting no response, he'd cursed them. He'd been instructed in what to do if such a thing happened to Cardigan, and, knowing he was already dead, he'd told himself to leave the mourning until later when he was alone. There were more important things to be doing, one of them trying to lift the heavy body into the back of the car.

As Sam worked, he'd sweated and breathed heavily. Hefting Cardigan up by the armpits, he'd propped him against the back wing of the car, opened the back door, and unceremoniously heaved the top half of the body onto the back seat, leaving the legs dangling out. He'd rushed to the other side and dragged Cardigan in.

Now, sitting parked a street away, his boss's body behind him under a blanket from the boot, he reckoned he'd have to ring Debbie.

*Shit.*

He took his phone out and sighed. She'd know, with his name coming up on her screen, that things weren't good. He was only meant to phone her if Cardigan couldn't.

Sam selected her number and pressed the icon to connect the call.

"No," she said as soon as she answered.

"I'm sorry, Deb." He felt a right bastard, but if he hadn't contacted her, Cardigan would haunt him. "It went a bit wrong."

"How much is a bit?"

"He's dead, love."

Debbie's scream hurt his eardrum, but he kept the phone pressed close, her grief entering him and joining with his own. She cried for a while, then calmed and sniffed.

"What am I going to do without him?" she asked.

He'd told Cardigan that Debbie had got too attached, but he hadn't realised how much. Sam had suspected she'd only shagged his friend to save herself getting in the shit with him if she refused, and maybe that was true at first. But now? Fuck, she loved him.

"Keep going," Sam said. "It's all you can do. Enjoy The Angel like he would have wanted."

Now he fully understood why Ron had given it to her. A reward for loving someone who'd never quite loved her enough back, the ghost of his late wife still flying through his veins. But Ron had done right by Debbie, and she'd see, once the initial shock had worn off, that he'd loved her in his own way, and giving her the pub had shown it.

Much as he felt sorry for the poor cow, he had shit to do, so he gently reminded her of that and ended the call. He'd hidden here for long enough. Any nosy bastards would just see the blood on the ground and shrug it off. He needed to do some damage control in case a copper came by, so he got out and walked back to the flats, looking around. A net curtain twitched, and he went to that house, knocking on the door. Some time passed, then the occupant opened up, chain in place. The woman was in her thirties. A straggle of children hid behind her skirts and peeped at Sam.

"I haven't seen anything," she said. "I don't want anything to do with this." She made to shut the door.

He put his hand out to prevent it from closing, and she glared at him.

"What d'you want? I told you, you haven't got to worry about me. I didn't see a thing."

Sam held his hand up. "It's all right, love. All I want is a bucket of hot soapy water to clean the path; otherwise, you'll be getting questions asked."

"But I don't want any involvement."

Impatient, Sam sighed and glanced from left to right. "The more fuss you make, the more attention you'll bring to yourself. I promise you, you won't get any bother from the police. Unless you've got any do-good neighbours?"

"You've got to be bloody joking. No one does any good around here." She paused for a moment, hand to chin. "Hold on while I fill the bucket. Will you need a scrubbing brush?"

"If you wouldn't mind." Sam felt exposed and unsafe on the doorstep. He nosed about. No one seemed to be around. The gunshot would have seen to that. He turned back to the woman.

"No, I don't mind," she said, "but I don't want it back after you've been scrubbing that poor sod's blood."

Sam tried to smile understandingly. She appeared tired and worn-out from living in poverty, from what he could tell. She obviously had a hand-to-mouth existence, although she and the children appeared clean and well cared for. "Just hurry up."

She smiled, cheeks flushed, and bustled off, leaving her three children standing near the door.

*They all look like a good dinner would go down a treat. Some new clothes wouldn't go amiss either.*

Sam was reminded of his early childhood, when he and his family had nothing to speak of, and his mother had to go out to work all the hours God sent to feed and clothe him and his brothers.

His heart strings tugged. He reached into his pocket and gave some money to the eldest child. "Make sure you share it out."

The lad took the cash and continued to stare at Sam. He then gawped down at the money and didn't seem to comprehend just how much was there. His mother returned, and the boy fisted the cash.

"I've filled it with hot water and splashed a bit of disinfectant and washing-up liquid in it. The brush is in there somewhere, so mind you don't burn your hands." She looked down at her children.

The boy opened his hand and showed her the money.

"Where did you bloody get that lot?" she asked, her cheeks flushing darker.

"That bloke gave it us. Said we had to share it."

She smiled at Sam, eyes bright and shiny.

He stood, uncomfortable under her scrutiny.

Then she said, "Don't forget, I don't want those back."

"I'll take it with me, don't panic. Here, have some money to buy a new bucket and brush." He thrust some notes at her. "I don't know how much they cost these days."

"Fucking Nora, are your minted or something?"

"I'm just grateful you've helped me. I won't forget it."

Sam took a deep breath and returned to the path. After he cleaned the blood, he got into Cardigan's car and drove away, mentally reminding himself of the woman's address.

His mind turned to other matters. He'd have to act fast in order to get Cardigan's death certificate. No police were to be involved—his boss' express orders.

There was only one place he could go.

Leona's.

# Chapter Forty-Three

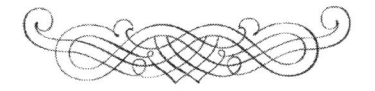

Debbie sat on the floor in her bedroom and cried until her body felt like it weighed a tonne. All the energy had gone out of her with every tear she'd shed, but they'd dried up, leaving her eyes gritty and sore.

How had she fallen so deeply for Cardigan? It was only now she realised how much she cared about him. People thought it was weird, a younger woman with a much older man, her the possible gold digger only pretending to give a shit about him so he didn't hurt her. But that wasn't true.

For the first few times with him, she'd been wary, but his manner around her wasn't the same as the man she'd previously known. He laughed a lot, was caring, always cuddling her before and after sex, none of this dipping his wick then fucking off until next time. They'd shared late-night phone calls, slowly revealing more of themselves, and when he'd made the switch from her going to his house to her running The Angel, everything had changed.

He'd become more attentive, giving her his full focus, and she'd done the same. Every so often, after her shift, she'd found him waiting at the top of the steel steps outside her flat, a grin on display in the moonlight, and those times she pretended they were a proper couple. He moved around her place as if he belonged there, and more than once she wanted to tell him he did.

Instead, she'd kept her mouth shut, unsure if his feelings for her were the same as hers for him. When he'd told her The Angel was hers, she'd known then. He might not have loved her like he had his wife, but he'd cared deeply.

Life without him wouldn't be the same, but she'd just have to get on with it like he would've wanted. She'd work hard and make the pub an even bigger success. He'd smile from wherever he was, and she'd comfort herself with that.

The only thing she needed to know was the story of how he'd died. There was no way he'd want anyone knowing he'd got stabbed or shot. There'd be some other reason why Cardigan was no longer around.

And as for Mickey, he'd better watch his back. She was gunning for him.

# Chapter Forty-Four

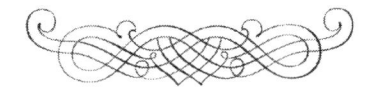

Leona had another letter.

Seeing the cream envelope lying on the mat as she'd walked down the stairs had her stomach contracting. The writer was telling her a story of some kind, like she'd guessed. The sentences she'd so far received would spell out what the sender really wanted to say. Eventually. Or, the sender would slip up some time, and then Leona would know who'd written them.

### FROM LITTLE ACORNS, OAK TREES GROW

Frustrated and angry, she went into the kitchen and drummed the worktop with her fingertips, irritating herself by mimicking her father.

A rustling noise sounded, coming through the open window behind her. The rustle came again, but she dared not turn round. Her chest felt like it was being crushed and squeezed. She struggled to take a deep breath and placed her hands on her throat. Her lungs would only allow so much air in, and her head spun. Someone knocked on the window. She screamed—a piercing one that hurt her ears.

A man called her name.

"Go away," she shouted, blood pulsing.

"Leona, it's me."

Relief. Total and utter relief.

*Sam.*

Why was he at the back window, in the bushes?

She moved that way. He peered through the net curtains, so she flung them aside. Sam stood in the middle of one of her wonderfully pruned shrubs, dishevelled, his white shirt covered in blood.

Blood! Had the note sender tried to hurt him, too?

Confused and unsure of what to do, she said, "What's happened?"

"Go to the back door, love. Quickly."

Sensing the urgency in Sam's voice, she lost no time in racing there. She unlocked and swung it wide. He came into view and beckoned her out into the garden.

"Come and help me. Leave the door open."

Puzzled and frightened, she went in Sam's wake, out to her father's car parked in her drive, close to the back of the house. He opened one of the rear doors and pulled out a body.

*Oh no. I'm not having anything to do with this.*

Indignation tightened her chest. She opened her mouth to protest, but no sound emerged.

Sam heaved, grunted, and dragged the body towards her.

She took a sharp intake of breath.

It was her father.

# Chapter Forty-Five

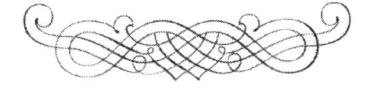

"It's me, Mickey. I'm back, safe and bloody sound."

Harry breezed into the living room, his face set in the biggest smile Mickey had ever seen on the bloke. Swaggering over to the settee, Harry plonked himself down and then promptly got up again to pour a stiff drink.

"What took you so long?" Mickey had been uneasy the whole time his mate had been out, his nerves shredded.

"I had a chat with the twins before I came home," Harry said, beaming.

*The twins? Christ.* "What? Start from the bloody beginning. Did you kill Cardigan?"

"I did. Drink?"

Mickey nodded, his mind going haywire. *Fuck me, he's really pulled it off.*

Harry poured another whiskey. He sat and passed Mickey his glass, telling the tale of the last two hours.

Mickey couldn't get over the news. "What were The Brothers doing wanting to do Cardigan over?"

It didn't seem possible. You didn't cut off your nose to spite your face, did you. Where would they get the majority of their wages from now? Cardigan must have really got on their nerves for them to want to kill him.

Harry gulped the amber liquid. "They'd had enough of him telling them what to do, I suppose. Dunno really, I didn't poke into it. They said they're taking over the patch. They asked me to give them a lift back to their van, and I went and had a look out the front of the flats to see if the pigs had been called."

Mickey swallowed the rest of his drink in one gulp. "And had they?"

"Not a rasher in sight, mate. I'd say I'm home and dry, and I've got rid of one of the biggest wankers around."

Doubt roiled inside Mickey. "Are you sure The Brothers aren't just stringing you along? They might come after you later down the line. Or that bloody Sam. He won't take kindly to what happened." He rubbed his chin from the worry of it all. "And what about me? We heard they still weren't happy with just breaking my leg and fucking up my face."

Harry shrugged. "The twins are all right. And as for Sam, I reckon he'll think they did it. We'll be all right, you'll see. Anyway, if I do see Sam, I'll tell him I was late coming with the money, and when I turned up, no fucker was there."

"As long as you're sure everything's sewn up. I want to be able to sleep in my bed at night."

"Sleep away, mate. I'm not going anywhere, least of all prison."

# Chapter Forty-Six

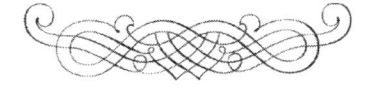

Leona came round in her bedroom. Out of sorts and wondering what she was doing in bed at this time of day, she frowned. Then reason the came crashing down on her.

Sam in the bushes.
Going to the car.
Her father's body.

A bullet wound to the head.

Everything going black.

She gritted her teeth to stave off crying and glanced at the clock on the nightstand. She'd only been asleep for forty-five minutes. Was that someone chatting in the spare room? She got up and went to her bedroom door. Opened it slightly. Sam was talking to someone.

She crept out into the hallway to the spare room door, which was ajar.

"I can take the bullet out and do some sort of job on the forehead, although there'll be a slight dent even after I've finished. I'll pack out the back of the head. Doing it here isn't satisfactory either, but there's not a lot we can do about that," a man said, his voice educated.

A voice that set Leona's heart beating faster. *Doctor Rushton.*

"And the death certificate?" Sam asked. "Can you sort that out?"

Rushton sighed. "I could put it down to a heart attack, I suppose. All that alcohol and cigars can't have been good for him. You shouldn't have any problems."

"I need to check with his daughter. He left some instructions. I knew to contact you, but I haven't got a clue about anything else."

"I think you'll find that the funeral director I was going to suggest is the one Mr Cardigan would have wanted. He came to visit me a couple of days ago, and I've been waiting for this to happen. He seemed to know. Told me what to do." There was a brief pause. "Right, I'll go and get my bag and tidy him up a bit."

Leona leant on the doorframe. In shock, eyes wide and stomach rolling, she placed her hand over her mouth to stop any noise escaping.

Rushton came out and stopped short, staring at her, his wrinkles prominent beside his eyes. "Leona. I'm sorry about your father. Is there anything I can do for you? Not feeling distraught after you fainted? Need a sedative?"

She ignored his questions. "I didn't know...I didn't think you were the type to do this. What would they say at the hospital? I-I won't be able to visit there anymore."

"Don't be silly," Rushton said, greying hair smoothed back with gel, handlebar moustache expertly shaped. "Of course you'll be able to visit the patients. Nobody will know what I've done here today. I can't imagine you'll be telling anyone, can you?" He rubbed his protruding stomach with both hands.

Leona blushed. How had things come to this? A well-respected doctor at the hospital where she did her charitable duty was really someone who covered up suspicious deaths on the quiet.

"No," she said. "I won't be telling anyone. And thank you for taking your time to do this, for someone you hardly know."

"On the contrary, me and your father are old acquaintances. There's been many a time when my services were needed where his work was concerned." He smiled, nudging her, and gave a conspirator's wink. "It's just unfortunate that I'm ministering to him in his death instead of ministering to Mr Cardigan's victims in theirs. But such is life, it's never as it seems." Patting her on the arm, he made to go down the stairs. He looked back at her, hand on the newel post. "I must push on now, get my bag before it's impossible to work on your father. A cup of tea wouldn't go amiss, though."

Shocked by the ordinariness in which he was taking the situation, she understood there was a lot more she didn't know about her father. He'd never once said he knew Doctor Rushton when she'd mentioned him. Much as it grated, she'd have to accept his services.

*But Sam can deal with that side of things.*

She stepped into the spare room, averting her eyes from her father lying on the bed under one of her pure-white starched sheets. She wouldn't be using *that* one again.

"What happened?" she asked Sam.

"He got shot in the head."

"I can see that," she snapped. "But how—and why?"

"Someone owed him money. He went to meet them, they were going to pay it back. They never showed. Someone shot him. That's it."

"That's it? He's been shot and is now dead, all because someone didn't want to pay him back what they owed? And all you can say is: That's it!"

Sam sighed. "They didn't exactly owe him the money, though. They won it off him fair and square, and he didn't like it. So he wanted it back."

"He wouldn't have done that. If they won it, he would have let them have it. I won't have you putting him down."

Sam looked at her sadly. "I've known him for years, you know that. Right from when we were nippers. He did things that made even me squirm, but I stuck by him because he was the only person who ever made me feel good. He understood me and gave me support and encouragement. I'm not trying to make him look bad now he's dead, I'm just stating the facts. You know I wouldn't slag him off, saying stuff that wasn't true. He wanted that money back, and nothing was going to stop him. I knew this job was a bad one right from the start, but he wouldn't listen."

Chagrined, Leona said, "I'm sorry. I shouldn't have said what I did."

"We'll put it down to grief, shall we?"

She had no one now, except Jonathan. And what sort of solace was that? He'd probably be off and running once he knew her father was dead. Unless she explained *she'd* now be buying the beer. *If I keep the pubs.*

"I'll be down in a minute. Rushton's got work to do," Sam said, breaking her out of her thoughts.

"I have." Rushton bustled into the room. "So I suggest you make yourself scarce…unless you like the sight of blood."

He chuckled and went down quickly in Leona's estimation.

Leaving the room with Sam, she went to the kitchen to make a pot of tea. Sam could take the doctor a cup. She wasn't going in there again in a hurry. At the kitchen table, her body heavy, she waited for the kettle to boil, glancing over at Sam who leant on the sink unit staring out of the window.

"I don't know what I'm going to do now," he said.

Leona's eyes pricked. "Will you retire, do you think?"

"I won't work for anyone else. Yeah, I'm going to give this lark up."

"So you're not going to find whoever did this?" Leona waved her arms.

"Nah. I'm no good without Ron. I'm not playing this game anymore. I'm too old. Enough's enough, eh?"

Leona calmed. "I agree." She gazed wistfully at the trees beyond the glass, remembering. "My father came to see me, you know. He must have known this was a dangerous job. He talked about his will and that I'd get all the pubs. He asked that I don't sell The Eagle to strangers."

Sam turned and smiled at her. "Yeah, he loved that boozer."

"Are you arranging the funeral and everything?"

"That doctor'll do it. He's in with the director. Leave it all to him."

"Drink your tea, Sam." She handed one to him. "And thank you for what you've done today. I would have phoned the police in a panic."

"In our line of work, the police don't even come into it. Your dad wouldn't want coppers involved. So I did what I could. I wouldn't have done anything less." A tear spilled down his face. "Because I loved him like a brother."

# Chapter Forty-Seven

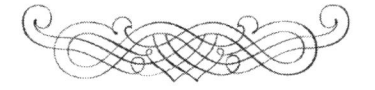

Jonathan swerved the car onto the drive in Vandelies Road. Two more cars were down the side of the house. He got out of his and walked over to the others. The one he'd parked behind wasn't familiar, but the first one was Cardigan's. That was another thing he could do without, his loud-mouthed father-in-law getting his back up.

The day was going from bad to worse.

He entered the house. Nothing seemed off. No voices.

*Where are they?*

"Leona?" he called, going into the kitchen and then the dining room, finding no one. The lounge was empty, too. He climbed the stairs. Mumbled voices came from one of the rooms. On the landing, he went past each door, cocking an ear.

The voices came from the spare room.

*What the fuck's going on?*

He knocked quietly.

Leona said, "That must be Jonathan home. I'll just explain."

The door opened enough for her to squeeze through the gap. She closed it behind her and looked at him. Then her eyes darted left to right.

"Explain what?" he said.

"My father died of a heart attack today," she replied bluntly.

"Bloody hell…" Jonathan puffed out his breath. *He's fucking dead. What a result.*

Leona gritted her teeth and grimaced. "Would you like to see him after the doctor has signed the death certificate? He's in there now with Sam."

He shook his head and turned away from her and, going downstairs, tried to hide his elation at the news. There he was, worrying all afternoon about what to do to get away from Leona, and all along, Cardigan was dying of a heart attack.

*And I don't feel bad. He meant nothing to me. He was just a bully and a criminal who deserves to be cold and dead.*

In the kitchen, he made himself a quick bite to eat. Voices came from the hallway. Sam, Leona, and what he supposed was the doctor.

*He must be leaving.*

"Goodbye, Doctor Rushton, and you, too, Sam," Leona said.

A male mumbled.

Leona: "Yes, I'll expect them shortly. And thank you…for everything."

"You're welcome," the doctor said.

The front door closed, and Leona came through into the kitchen.

"Death doesn't affect your appetite then?" she said spitefully.

"Well, you've got to eat, haven't you, whether someone's dead or not."

"You're such an insensitive man. I should never have agreed to marry you. It's brought me nothing but aggravation."

"We can split now your father's dead, get an annulment, so don't worry about it. You can get back to the life you had before I came along and spoiled it."

*The quicker the better.*

Leona smiled. "Oh, by the way, are you going to be running off with that Rebecca woman now?"

Frustrated, Jonathan sighed. "I told you, I haven't been seeing her. I just want to be free to get on with my life. And you can get on with yours."

She held her finger to her lips. "I'll have to think about it. I'll be the one buying the beer. Without me doing that, your business will fold. Shame." She marched off.

Jonathan followed. "I'm going out," he shouted and opened the front door.

"But I thought you wanted to see my father," Leona called from halfway up the stairs.

"No, thanks. I've got better things to do."

Her cheeks stained pink. "Well, the least you could do is show your respect."

Jonathan sighed again and closed the front door. Wearily walking up the stairs, he followed her to the spare room. She opened the door and held it. He went in. The door closed behind him.

"Pull the sheet back then," Leona said, impatient.

Jonathan approached the bed, tentatively holding the corner of the sheet. He pulled it back as far as Cardigan's shoulders. Stared at his former father-in-law. Something about his face wasn't right.

"Are you sure he died of a heart attack, Leona?"

She took a sharp intake of breath, and he turned to look at her.

She covered her mouth, a crimson flush over her cheeks. "Of course I'm sure. Just what are you insinuating?"

"You tell me. This isn't any heart attack, and I wasn't born yesterday. You'd better tell that doctor he hasn't done a very good patch-up job."

"Patch-up job? He just came and issued a death certificate. He'd only been here a short while before you turned up."

He jerked a thumb towards Cardigan. "If he had a heart attack, it must have been as he was going down after being shot. Your father's got a slight dent in his forehead, and I'd bet he doesn't own a back to his head now."

Leona shook.

"And that dent, Leona, is suspiciously like a covered-up bullet hole."

# Chapter Forty-Eight

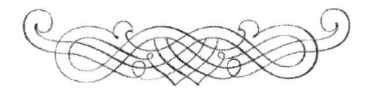

The church had been packed to bursting. So much so that some had to stand at the back. Others huddled in the doorway, one against the other. Now the graveside was five deep with grievers, all there to say their last goodbyes to Ronald Arthur Cardigan.

Many of the criminal fraternity attended, and a heavy police presence filled the paths—maybe they suspected he'd been killed. A K9 dog sat patiently, panting next to its master. Cardigan had many friends as well as enemies. Those who weren't on good terms with him were there to make sure he really *was* dead.

Jonathan hid a smile.

He stood behind Leona at the graveside, her head bent and shoulders drooping as the vicar went through the motions. He envisaged his life once this day was over. He'd file for an annulment and put the brewery up for sale tomorrow. Cardigan dying had given him a new lease of life, so he thanked his lucky stars for Harry and Mickey having the guts to go through with the killing. Sonny had told Jonathan about it. Apparently, Cardigan would want it kept under everyone's hats, so Sonny's source had said, so no one was to spread the news.

*I just want this over with.*

He looked around at all present. Leona, Debbie, Sam, Jack, and Cardigan's other close friends seemed to be the only ones showing genuine remorse. George and Greg Wilkes stood, heads bent, shoulders broad, their faces grim and menacing. Pub landlords, who Jonathan knew only by sight, had also come to pay their respects to a boss who'd let them have free rein on running his establishments—providing they kept their mouths shut about what went on in the back rooms. Or out the back of The Angel—everyone knew about the tarts there. Said tarts had chosen decent clothes for today instead of their scanty shit. One cried in the extreme. Debbie. He knew her from school.

*Surely they're all wondering what to do now. Their jobs are on the line, especially if Leona sells the pubs.*

Mickey and Harry stood at the rear of the crowd, Harry seeming smug and Mickey on edge. He darted his head back and forth, staring over at the police dog.

*He won't be able to run very far if they chase him. Heard his leg still plays him up.*

Jonathan turned back to the grave. Leona threw a white rose and some loose earth into Cardigan's last resting place. From the corner of his eye, Jonathan caught Harry and Mickey leaving, getting into a car and driving away, the exhaust smoke billowing out. Another car moved slowly towards the mass of two hundred or more people huddled together. It belonged to someone he knew, and he hoped the person driving here wasn't the owner.

It was Gracie's.

Debbie hadn't expected to be standing beside another grave so soon after being by Shirley's, yet here she was, looking down into the hole, a coffin inside it containing the man her soul had loved but hadn't had the decency to let her fully in on it. Mud marred the lid, clumps of it scattered across the gold-coloured plaque, obscuring some letters of his name.

Cardigan's daughter had stared at Debbie a lot during the service in the church but ignored her now. Debbie was glad. The woman had a mean air about her, and she was probably giving Debbie evils because she thought Cardigan had left everything to her.

*No, just The Angel.*

Iris put her arm around Debbie and led her away. Lavender and Lily, plus a lot of other girls who worked the corners, drifted with them. There was a clause in the papers regarding The Angel, saying Debbie had to 'look after' people with Cardigan gone. He'd meant the girls, all of them, not just those at the parlour. Cardigan had been their pimp, but not the mean sort, and he wanted them to still have a rudder in her. He'd arranged a 'trust fund', and she'd receive money to employ men to help her out. She'd find some to stand watch on the corner, pay them from the fund, but she wasn't about to take a cut of the girls' earnings like Cardigan had.

She couldn't bring herself to do that, not when she didn't need the money. He'd turn in his grave over it, but she had to do what her conscience allowed.

Debbie and the girls walked from the cemetery, up Shirley's road, and around the corner. In The Angel, she instructed Lisa to pour drinks on the house for anyone who hadn't been invited back to Cardigan's place. His daughter had arranged the wake, and the likes of Debbie and her customers weren't welcome.

That was all right, she didn't want to go there anyway. She'd send her fella off in her own way, holding back the tears and smiling.

After all, that was what he'd have wanted.

---

Standing by the car, Rebecca observed the many people now leaving the graveside. The straggle that were left waited for the deceased's daughter, and that was just who Rebecca herself waited for.

Her mind wandered back to William's burial here. Leona had shown up when the coffin was being lowered into the gaping hole, and Rebecca had seen her, mortified.

She peered through half-lidded eyes at her old friend. Leona had tainted William's funeral for Rebecca, and as soon as she'd heard from Jonathan that Ronald Cardigan was dead, she'd lost no time in finding out when the funeral was.

Musing on the strength of the hate she harboured for that woman, Rebecca wondered if she was bordering on insane with regards to the hurt she wanted her rival to feel. Rival. Did she really still think of her like that?

Leona had aged terribly, dowdy and appearing ten years older.

*She never was an oil painting.*

Leona walked away from the grave. She stopped suddenly and glanced upwards, tilting her head as if to listen, then turned in Rebecca's direction. They stared hard at one another, Leona's face showing shock and horror amongst the grief. Her mouth formed an 'O' of surprise.

Rebecca got back in the car. She'd succeeded in doing what she'd set out to do: hurt Leona. Putting on her seat belt, she continued to stare at the woman, humming.

"I feel another letter coming on."

Seeing that it was Rebecca and not Gracie who'd got out of the car to gaze over at the mourners gave Jonathan much relief. Was she up to something by coming here?

Not knowing what to think, he watched from inside the safety of the head funeral car. Leona and Sam walked towards it. Rebecca drove at her. As Leona reached the wide road that skirted the cemetery, Rebecca stopped to let her pass. Leona refused to walk across. Rebecca waved to Sam, who held Leona's elbow. Sam tried to propel Leona onwards, but she held her ground.

Jonathan inched the window down.

"I will *not* cross in front of that bitch's car. She might try to run me over."

Sam tried to cajole Leona again. "You don't even know her. Just walk so we can get to the wake. Come on, love."

"No. Tell her to drive on."

Sam shook his head. "Go on, woman." He gesticulated at Rebecca to get the message over.

Rebecca moved forward, slowly, an inch or two.

Leona's eyes widened. "Tell her to go away. She's opening the window."

Smiling, Rebecca drove out of the cemetery.

Leona got into the car next to Jonathan. "Your girlfriend couldn't resist coming here just to spite me, could she, the cow."

Annoyed she was still thinking along those lines, he clamped his mouth shut. Tense and uptight that Rebecca had dared to show up here today at all, and his mind whirling with the thoughts that he'd at last be free of this insane woman, he said, "If I've told you once, I've told you a thousand times, Rebecca is not my girlfriend. I don't know what she was bloody doing here. Probably to get on your nerves, and she's succeeded."

Sam got in the car, and he drove back to Ronald Cardigan's house in silence.

Peace, at last.

# Chapter Forty-Nine

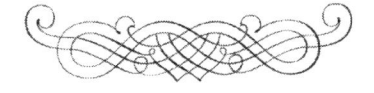

Rebecca sat at her desk, newspapers scattered in front of her, glue and scissors at the ready. What could she say to really put the wind up Leona? She rested her hands under her chin and had a good, hard think. She'd already sent a note hinting at Gracie's pregnancy—her daughter didn't think she knew, but she'd guessed.

*Ronald Cardigan's death was suspicious. It had to be something more than a heart attack.*

She cut out the letters she needed for what she wanted to say and laid them on the page.

They looked quite chilling.

Once it was dry, she walked to the postbox.

---

Two days after she'd buried her father, Leona received another letter. She didn't need this sort of thing today. She'd been going around in a stupor, dazed, the shock of what had happened finally sinking in.

Picking up the post, she went into the lounge and curled her feet underneath her. She opened the dreaded letter.

HEART ATTACK? WE KNOW BETTER, DON'T WE, LEONA?

Tears fell down her cheeks and into the crook of her neck. She tasted the saltiness of them as they ran past her lips. Was this ever going to end? Were they going to torment her for the rest of her life? It *must* be someone who knew her father. Maybe even whoever had killed him. They were trying to scare her.

She rose and threw the thing in the fire. The flames devoured the page, and in some sort of purposeful rage, she went to the locked drawer and retrieved the other notes. She dashed them into the fire, too, crying away the frustration and anger she'd been experiencing.

# Chapter Fifty

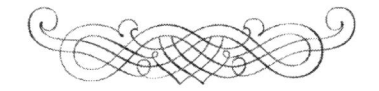

In The Eagle, Jonathan was well and truly away with the fairies, drunk on scotch after scotch. He idly listened to Fiona chatting to another customer.

"Well, Jack'll be a while yet. He's gone to Cardigan's grave," she said to Stanley, an old man at the end of the bar. "They were good friends, him and Ron. He's meeting his mates after. The wake seems to have reunited them all. I shouldn't wonder if Jack comes rolling in about two in the morning."

"Heart attack, you said?" Stanley spluttered through the gaps in his teeth.

Fiona nodded. "Yeah. Shame, eh? He did drink some, though. That couldn't have helped."

"I heard different. Shot in the head, some say."

"Well, you can't believe everything you hear, can you? Gossip's the worst kind of thing you can listen to. The rumours concerning Ron are a load of rubbish. It stands to reason people are going to think he met a bad end. It doesn't look good that a gangland boss died legit."

Stanley sighed. "I don't care what you say. I believe he copped a bullet. But, search me as to who did it, because there's a pick of many a man who'd love to lay claim to that one."

"Hmm. His son-in-law's sinking a fair few tonight. Can't say I blame him. Not that I'm complaining, it's more money in the till. But who knows how long it'll be lining our pockets, because with Ron gone, no one knows whether his daughter'll keep the pubs up and running. I heard she's inherited the lot."

Jonathan gulped more scotch.

"She'll sell," Stanley said, spittle dripping down his chin.

"You're in a shitty mood tonight, Stanley." Fiona rolled her eyes.

"Well, I'm only saying what's true. She'll sell, and she won't give a tinker's cuss as to what happens to you. Maybe the new owners'll keep you on, but I doubt it. They'll want fresh landlords."

"Are you calling me and Jack stale?"

Jonathan gazed at a hazy-looking Fiona then gawped at the empty glass in front of him. The ice had melted to little bobbles. His head drooped, and nausea spread up his windpipe. A hard clap on the back had him feeling sick, and he turned to see who'd hit him.

"Blimey, I was beginning to think I wouldn't see you again," Sonny said. "Where you been, mate?"

Since Cardigan's death, Jonathan had taken to staying later and later in Gracie's company instead of visiting The Eagle. Sonny got no response except a watery smile.

"You're pissed as a fart."

"I know that. Came here to get away from...shit."

"Leona?" Sonny asked.

"Especially Leona. Life's a mess."

"And you've only just noticed? Bloody hell, it's been a mess for months. What you doing in here getting so legless?"

"Gracie's pregnant."

"Fucking Nora. What are you going to do about it? With Cardigan dead—"

"I know what I'm going to do about it. I'm going to go home and tell the old battle-axe that I'm definitely getting an annulment. Then I'm going to ask Gracie to marry me."

"I think it's time you went home, mate. I'll drive you. I'll take your car."

Vandelies Road was quiet when they arrived, the house in darkness. Sonny foraged in Jonathan's pocket, found his house keys, and helped him to the front door.

"Thanks, mate," Jonathan said and lurched inside to bed, wanting nothing more than to forget.

# Chapter Fifty-One

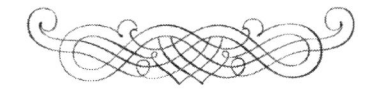

Throughout her teenage years, Gracie had envisaged getting married and having children with the man she loved. Well, she'd found the man she loved all right, and was pregnant with his baby, but she wasn't married. She'd been thinking about that all day at work, going into a daydream when the job she was doing had become boring.

Mum had been giving her funny looks each morning after Gracie was sick. Jonathan had been distant and preoccupied the last few days, and she'd put it down to the fact he didn't want her to have the baby, even though he'd said differently. He kept assuring her they'd get married, but not right now.

His excuse came to her: He wouldn't come to her penniless.

It didn't make sense, and she thought he was hiding something.

She had to go and see him later. Mum wanted them to go to some charity ball in December. Maybe she'd get him to open up then.

She felt sick.

"Are you okay?" Mum asked, coming into the kitchen.

Gracie rushed out of the room. On her knees in the downstairs loo, she hunched over the toilet.

"My cooking's not that bad, surely?" Rebecca laughed, leaning on the jamb.

Gracie sat back and, wiping her mouth with tissue, looked at her mother. "There's something I have to tell you."

"There's no need. I know."

# Chapter Fifty-Two

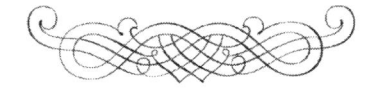

"I don't want to be married to you anymore," Jonathan said.

Shocked, Leona sneered, "Well, then, I'll stop ordering the beer, if it's all the same to you."

"Do what you like. I've had enough. I'm going to see a solicitor. I don't care about the poxy orders. There's only so much a bloke can take, and I've taken all I'm going to."

*What does he mean, he doesn't care about the orders?*

"You want to be with that Rebecca, don't you? It's her who's put you up to this. I knew she had a vendetta against me, but stealing my husband really takes the biscuit."

"You tried to steal hers," Jonathan spat. "Or is it one rule for you and another for everybody else? You make me sick. I should have refused to marry you."

"That's enough of that. I didn't try to steal William. We loved each other, and she took him away from me."

"You loved him, but he didn't love you. He loved her."

"Well, she would tell you that, wouldn't she. Your precious business going down the drain and you engaging in adulterous behaviour won't look too good when you try to divorce me."

"Non-consummation of marriage, your father being shot in the head, and you covering it up with the so-called Good Doctor Rushton, threatening me with all sorts… That won't look too good for *you*. I'll do whatever it takes to get rid of you."

Leona shook, and her head lightened. "You wouldn't dare."

"Wouldn't I? Just try me, woman."

Leona took a deep breath to steady her rapidly beating heart. She would *not* have her father's real death in the papers. She'd possibly go to prison for what she'd done, going along with the cover-up.

"Right, do what you like. I'll not contest it in any way," she said. "But it'll still take time. To get an annulment, I mean."

"However long it takes, I'll wait." He turned to leave.

"Where are you going?" she asked, eyes wide.

"Out. Not that it's any of your bloody business."

Leona narrowed her eyes, and all-consuming jealousy enveloped her. "Going to tell Rebecca all about it, are you? Going to let her know she's won?"

He walked out, slamming the door.

One thing she'd make sure of was whether Jonathan *was* having an affair with Rebecca. That was something she just had to know for her own peace of mind. She wouldn't rest until she knew the truth.

Pressure had lifted from Jonathan's shoulders as he'd left the marital home.

He'd gone to see a solicitor since then. The visit had been straight and to the point, and providing Leona agreed that they hadn't consummated their marriage, the annulment should be plain sailing. That had been good to hear, and he went to his house to wait for Gracie. He'd tell her she should keep the baby. He'd marry her once it had been born. Just how he was going to explain his reason for waiting, he didn't know. Perhaps there would be some kind of divine inspiration.

*Who knows?*

Gracie knocked on Jonathan's front door, and he answered it almost immediately. He must have been looking out for her from the window.

He appeared tense, and it hiked up her nerves.

In the small living room, she sat on the worn sofa and told herself to come straight out with it. "I'm going to keep our baby. I've been giving it a lot of thought, and I can't get rid of it."

He sat beside her and held her hands. "If I could explain why I can't marry you yet, I would. But I'll marry you when I can. It's impossible at the minute."

"There can't be anything that could stop us being together. Unless you're already married." She laughed.

Jonathan's face paled.

She stared at him. "Is that it? Are you married?"

He blinked, and she felt sick to her stomach.

*Why hadn't I ever realised?*

He squeezed her hands. "You don't understand. I only—"

"Save your breath. I'm not listening."

She ran from the house, got into her car, and drove away at top speed.

# Chapter Fifty-Three

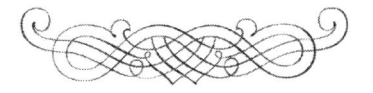

A month had passed since Cardigan's death, and Debbie had finally come out of the initial stages of grief. She'd been through the shock, upset, and anger, and now she was determined to live a full life, but before she did, she'd go and see Mickey. He'd come out of whatever hole he'd been hiding in, probably feeling safe now with Cardigan dead.

But he wasn't safe. Not by a long chalk.

She had everything sorted in her mind. The parlour girls had promised they'd have her back, saying she was with them, so her alibi was set.

Just in case.

---

Harry and Mickey had tried hard to find out who'd killed Shirley Richmond. It most definitely wasn't anyone in their circles, so they gave it up as being something they'd never know.

They'd come out of hiding on the day of the funeral, hearing through the grapevine that the identity of Cardigan's killer was uncertain. It could've been anyone, some said. The thing was, some undercurrent whispers said Mickey had done it, and Harry, being a selfish twat at times, hadn't put the gossipers right.

Going back to their former jobs as market traders and knock-off merchants, they kept a low profile all the same.

Just in case.

George and Greg had taken over the manor. They had the contacts, and people knew where to get hold of them. George had settled down since Cardigan's death, not wanting to inflict any more pain on a person than was necessary or requested. He was seeing a therapist.

"I'm glad we found out it wasn't Mickey who killed Shirley. I didn't really fancy beating him up again," Greg said.

"Yeah. Unless Harry was lying when he said Mickey hadn't left the safe house." George rubbed his chin.

"We'll put it down to her getting killed by a nasty punter. That's all it could have been. Poor cow."

They kept their eyes and ears open, though, as they might inadvertently find out who'd done it. Then they could confront them. So they scanned through the newspapers and kept an eye out.

Just in case.

Sam was taking a while to become accustomed to his retirement. Cardigan's death had been like a physical blow; he couldn't get over the fact he'd never see Ron again. Never be needed by the big man to escort him round in the car. Never be needed to help out when there was a bit of bother.

He'd had such a busy life with him, and now he had too much time on his hands. Time he spent sleeping the hours away, only to wake up and start the whole process again.

He hated the fact he had no oomph in him to go after Mickey. All the fight had left him with Cardigan's departure. He hoped his boss and friend would understand. And Sam also hated mornings. Another day where he had to find himself something to do, give his mind something to think about. He usually ended up going back through time, reliving the years Cardigan had ruled the manor. He supposed someone else would have taken their place already.

He didn't care about any of it.

Sighing, he wondered if he'd have changed any part of his life. Nah, he wouldn't. He would've done things exactly the same, except maybe known, somehow, that the bullet had been sailing through the air and he could have knocked Cardigan out of the way before it hit him.

All his reasons for breathing air into his lungs had gone. He wouldn't be long in following his master to the pearly gates.

He sat back in his leather chair, tried to keep his eyes open, wishing he'd slip away. The promises he'd made to people filtered through his mind. He recalled the woman with all the children, the one who'd given him the bucket and brush. Leaning forward, he swivelled along on his chair wheels and reached into his desk drawer. He had a purpose now. Something to do with his boring day.

He'd already rung the bank and requested a withdrawal, picking it up the next day.

The large padded envelope was sealed, its contents safe inside, the address on the front. He got up and put on his coat. It was only a walk to the end of the road where the little shop had a post office. He'd send it registered.

At least he'd kept that promise. He'd let Ron down, and would be letting Leona down, but the woman in the flats would soon find out Christmas had definitely come early for her and her family.

Janine had been used to eking out the food ever since she'd been married and had watched her mother do the same throughout her childhood.

Her husband, Kip, bent down and picked up the post. "There's a big padded envelope here, just addressed to The Occupants."

"Give it to me."

Tearing it open, Janine pulled out the contents. It was a wedge of something inside a folded piece of paper. She gasped in surprise when the wedge turned out to be thick bundles of notes held together with elastic bands. There had to be about two hundred thousand there. She held up her hand, silencing Kip, and read the note, tears spilling down her face. Once finished, she passed the letter to Kip.

*I'm sure you'll remember me as the man who borrowed the bucket. I just wanted to let you know how grateful I was for your help that day. There will be no hassle for what you did, and from the nature of my visit, you'll know my friend's death wasn't the usual, and for keeping your mouth shut, I'm grateful.*

*Take this money from me. I'm getting on a bit, so humour the old man, will you, and accept what I'm giving you in the good faith in which it's been sent.*

*I know you'll burn this letter when you've read it, but before you do, take note of my address at the top of the page and write and let me know your name.*

*I need to know it, see, to be able to leave you everything when I'm gone.*

*It may seem odd to you, for a total stranger to leave you and your family his money, but I have no one else, and to give it to you would give me no greater pleasure.*

*I'll tell you again, there's no hidden catch, and there's nothing you need do for the money. Just give them kids the best you can with it, and if you must in years to come, laugh about the nutty old fella who gave you a fortune for the loan of a scrubbing brush and bucket.*

*Good luck and happiness,*
*Sam*

---

Sam received the letter. Her name was Janine Felton, and she'd given details of her new address. Sam had done the right thing. He'd thanked her in the only way he knew how.

The new address had him smiling. Janine wasn't to know she'd bought a house that was dear to his heart. She didn't know she'd be living in a home he'd been in more than a thousand times.

Ron would have loved the irony of it.

Janine and her family had stepped up the ladder, more than a rung or two. They'd bought Ron's old house in Vandelies Road, probably using the money he'd sent as a deposit.

Once Sam had sent the relevant details to his solicitor, along with his request for a visit so he could write his final will and testament, admitting he was of sound mind and body, he felt lighter and happier than he had in a long time.

The end was near, and after the solicitor had gone and the papers had been signed and sealed, he lay his weary head on the pillow he'd taken to using while sitting in his leather chair.

He closed his eyes. Smiled. Feeling young again, he was going to meet Ron, where they'd be together once more. He was smiling because he wondered if God would be able to cope with the pair of them.

Rogues that they were.

# Chapter Fifty-Four

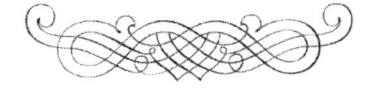

Having sold the house next door and putting the numerous public houses up for sale, Leona was ready to face her final mission. She'd received the annulment papers and signed them, sticking by her promise not to contest it in any way.

She was going to follow Jonathan and see if he met up with Rebecca. She had to know one way or the other if Rebecca had succeeded in winning the war.

She visited The Eagle and found out from Jack and Fiona that Jonathan lived just down the road. They expressed their sympathy that her marriage had been so short-lived. Leona basked in their apparent concern.

"I'm so sorry to have to sell the pubs, but I've come to tell you that The Eagle won't be one of the ones put on the market. My father had a particular fondness for this place, so if you'd like to stay, you're welcome. Not that I'd butt into the running of it, of course. Carry on as you've always done." She paused for a moment, thinking of what her father would've wanted. He'd said he didn't want the place going to *strangers,* so… "I tell you what, I hope you don't take this gesture the wrong way, but how about you two owning this place?"

Jack and Fiona looked at Leona, aghast.

"We wouldn't be able to afford it," Jack said. "Sorry, love, but we'll just have to settle for running it."

"You don't know what I mean, do you? I'm giving it to you."

"Giving?" Jack's eyes widened. "No, Leona, it's too generous an offer. We can't possibly—"

"You can. My father thought a lot of you, Jack. Take it as an inheritance from him. Please?"

Their beaming faces said it all.

"That's settled then. It's yours. I'll get all the necessary paperwork sorted out. Good luck to you." Leona swung out of the pub, feeling like a ten-foot goddess.

The next step in her plan was in place. She'd go to the market, much as it grated her, to buy some secondhand clothes. She'd dress up and follow Jonathan around for the day. Tomorrow would be good.

She found the shabby market situated not far from The Eagle. The air smelt different here, with its distinct cabbage odour. She shuddered as she rounded a corner, confronted by a sight she most abhorred: milling crowds poking around on the stalls.

She held her breath for as long as she could, and when she found herself bursting to breathe, she did so through her mouth so she wouldn't smell the disgusting winkles and cockles from the fishmonger's van.

She slitted her eyes and stomped straight to the secondhand clothes stall. She rummaged through the piles like someone possessed. What a fool she'd been, agreeing to marry *him*. At last, she found what she was looking for: an old tan rain mac, belted at the middle, which had definitely seen better days, and a floral scarf, large enough to wrap around her head and tie under the chin. She'd be giving *that* a good scrub before she let it anywhere near her hair.

---

The following morning, in the old clothing, Leona shuddered. As ready as she was ever going to be, she left the house, walking quickly in case any of the neighbours saw her in her get-up. She felt stupid in her disguise, but if a disguise was what it was, no one would know it was her, would they? She took out an old pair of her father's reading glasses, dark-framed and unflattering. She'd removed the lenses, as with them on she saw everything as if it were right in front of her.

She put her head down, her hands in her pockets, and arrived opposite The Eagle, hiding in a doorway. She held herself rigid when he emerged from his house right on time. She hoped he wouldn't use the car. It would be silly really, seeing that the brewery was only down the road and round the corner.

He walked off, much to her relief. She kept a discreet distance, frowning once he turned into the brewery gates. What had she expected? Not to have to wait around in the freezing cold, that was for sure. But wait she would. It was what she needed to do.

What if he left later and met Rebecca?

She'd deal with that if it came to it. No point in getting all het up until you had to, was there.

But Leona always got het up before she had to.

---

Jonathan left the brewery at lunchtime. On seeing Sonny enter The Eagle, he went to join his old friend for a quick drink.

"How's your head after I saw you last?" Sonny said.

"It's all right now, but the next day it was banging."

"Serves yourself right. It was self-inflicted. No sympathy for you."

"Hark at him, who must have a hangover every bloody day."

Sonny shook his head. "Nah, I drink in moderation, see. Never go over the top, that's my motto. Anyway, my missus wouldn't be happy seeing me staggering in of a night, pissed as a fart. I'm lucky she lets me out every evening as it is."

Jonathan took a long pull on his pint. "I told Leona I wanted shot of her. The annulment's going through at the moment."

"Thank God for that. Let's have another drink to celebrate."

"Just a pint. I'm not drinking whiskey again if I can help it."

---

So he spent his lunchtimes getting drunk, did he, while Leona visited poorly people in their hospital beds. Well, he'd be none of her concern soon.

She still huddled in the doorway, hungry. A car slowly came down the road. The same car that had stopped to let her pass at her father's funeral.

Shocked into stillness, she watched Jonathan come out of the pub and make his way towards the car. He opened the driver's door, and out came the woman who Leona despised more than anyone else in the world.

Rebecca Lynchwood.

*Wasn't I right all along? Didn't I say he'd been having an affair with her? Hadn't he blatantly denied it?*

Her anger rose as the pair of them went into Jonathan's house. Just what did they get up to in there?

As if she needed telling.

Now she knew the truth, she turned out of the doorway and headed for home, ripping the headscarf off and shoving it in her pocket. She snatched the glasses away from her face, giving the bridge of her nose immediate relief from where they'd been pinching, then she let herself break down. Sobs racked her body, and tears streamed. Passersby looked at her, some bewildered, some with sympathy, but all with the aloofness that said she was nothing to do with them.

# Chapter Fifty-Five

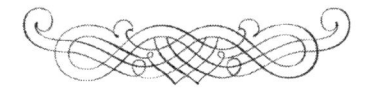

Mickey sat in front of Debbie in The Eagle. She'd already told Jack and Fiona her plan, and Jack especially was more than eager to help her out. Everyone on The Cardigan Estate knew who she was—gossip had gone round she was Cardigan's widow if only in name—and people respected her more now they knew he'd left her

The Angel. She had to be special for that to happen, so in his honour, they'd keep their traps shut about seeing her here if they knew what was good for them. One word from her to The Brothers, and they'd be silenced if they blabbed.

The twins had taken over, and good luck to them. The job suited them down to the ground.

"What do you want?" Mickey glanced about, shifty, as if he sensed a trap.

She'd have to steer him clear him of that notion.

Until she wanted to enlighten him.

She smiled her Peony smile. "With Cardigan and Shirley gone, I got to thinking."

He stiffened and looked at her, wary. "What about?"

"We're at loose ends, you and me."

"Eh?"

"You used to fuck Shirley, I fucked Cardigan." She shrugged. "If you're not interested…" She made to get up and leave.

He flashed his arm out and gripped her wrist. "Wait. I get what you're saying now."

She smiled again, despite internally cringing at Mickey's scar. It was worse than Shirley's. Whoever had sewn it up did a shit job. She leant forward to whisper, all for show. "We can't do anything at our own places." She paused. "Or the parlour. People would have my guts for garters if they saw us together. They'd say I was dancing on Cardigan's grave."

Mickey darted his gaze to Jack, who stood behind the bar staring at them.

"So why meet here then, you daft cow?" Mickey frowned. "Jack's the last person who ought to cop an eyeful of us."

She lowered her sights to his hand around her wrist. "Maybe you shouldn't be doing that."

He took it away.

"And besides," she went on, "he thinks I'm here to ask you about killing Cardigan."

Mickey reared back, eyes wide. "It fucking wasn't me."

She pretended to believe him. "Do you think I'd offer you a shag or ten if I thought it was?"

He relaxed. "Suppose."

She laughed quietly.

"What's so bleedin' funny?" he asked.

"It's just that Jack has no idea how I'm going to play him. How *we're* going to play him."

"What do you mean? I hate being kept in the dark, so spit it out."

"We're going to shag in his cellar."

"What?" Mickey said that a bit too loudly.

"Shh. He thinks I'm going to take you down there and force the truth out of you, but we know better, don't we." She gave him another Peony smile, the type she'd only ever reserved for Cardigan—and hated herself for it, but needs must.

"So what happens when we both come back upstairs? He'll want to know what I said."

"I'll say I don't think it was you, that someone else killed Cardigan. Bloody simple really. You get off scot-free, and me and you can be left alone to meet up in secret. I quite fancy an illicit affair, don't you, something only me and you know about. And don't go telling Harry either. I don't want him knowing my business."

Mickey grinned, his second smile lifting in a macabre way. "Yeah, I could do with a bit of excitement. Come on then."

Debbie could have danced. Mickey was so bloody gullible. Like she'd ever want to shag him. Still, his cock was doing the talking at the minute, so she led the way to the door marked PRIVATE, giving Jack an obvious nod so Mickey would think she was doing what she'd promised the landlord.

She led the way down a corridor, then opened a door on the left. The smell of the cold cellar seeped out, plus the hum of the machines in there. She moved down the stairs. A glance to the right told her two men hid, crouched behind a stack of silver barrels beneath a tarpaulin so Mickey didn't clock them. Jack had let them know someone would need disposing of, and they were more than happy to do it.

What she'd have to do next soured her stomach, but she'd done it before, separating herself from what she was doing with the many men she'd entertained, going to that safe haven inside her head where nothing could touch her, only coming back into the real world once they'd finished pawing her.

She waited for him at the bottom of the steps, anger rising at his smug grin. The hiss of a mechanism releasing and beer chugging through a pipe into the pump on the bar was a sound she'd forever associate with this moment. She was here, avenging Cardigan's death, and if it was the last thing she ever did, she'd die a happy woman.

"What do you like?" she asked when Mickey stood in front of her.

"A blow job would be nice. Best to do something quick to seal the deal. I don't fancy getting too engrossed, what with Jack being upstairs. He could come down any minute."

"He won't. I told him to give me time."

"Still, just suck me off."

Perfect. She lowered to her knees, getting busy, and while Mickey was off wherever he went inside his head when he had sex, she felt in her bag for the knife. Curled her fingers around the handle. Glanced up to make sure he had his eyes closed.

They were.

She eased her mouth off him and positioned the blade. Took him in hand instead. And sliced that fucker clean off.

His screams were the best kind of music, the type that got your blood pumping, happiness flowing through you. She stood with his piece of flesh in one hand, the knife in the other, and stared at him.

He covered his groin, crying, gasping, looking down at his hands covered in blood then back up at her in shock. "What…what the fuck, Deb?" Each word came out as separate sobs.

She stabbed him in the face, again and again, so fast he didn't have time to raise his hands to stop her. Then he did, and she took that moment to plunge the knife in the area of his heart. He staggered backwards, his shirt turning crimson, his cheeks ribbons of skin and claret, and fell against a barrel. Down he went onto the concrete floor, his blood staining it, pumping out of his chest to cover all the material on show between the fronts of his jacket.

For a moment he just stared at her, mouth working as if he had so much to say but his tongue wasn't helping him out to speak the words. Good, she didn't want to hear anything from him except the death rattle.

"That's for killing Cardigan," she said. "An eye for an eye, isn't that what he used to say?"

"It..." A red arc spurted from his mouth, staining his teeth, his chin.

"Save it. I'm not fucking interested."

"Wasn't..."

Then he took a shuddery breath, and it came back out twice as shaky, a wheeze accompanying it. She moved closer, knelt in front of him, and leant forward so his final breath went right in her ear. He took a sip of air, but it didn't make a return journey.

She smiled, imagined Cardigan saying, "Thanks, Treacle", and let the tears fall.

Debbie sat like that for maybe a minute, then stood and retreated a few steps.

"You can come out now," she said, turning in the direction of the barrels where the men hid.

The tarpaulin rustled, and The Brothers appeared, coming over to stand beside her. They stared over at Mickey.

"Oh, fuck me," George said.

"Bollocks," Greg muttered.

"What?" Debbie looked from one to the other.

"I heard you say to him this was for killing Cardigan." George scrubbed at his chin.

"Yes…" She stood tall, proud of what she'd done.

"Slight problem," George said.

Debbie frowned and shoved her hands on her hips. "Why?"

Greg and George peered at each other, as if reading what the other was thinking. "It wasn't him," they said together.

And Debbie's rage exploded. "You fucking what? *Everyone's* saying it was him."

"It wasn't." George shook his head. "Still, we'll clear up the mess, per the plan."

"How do you know it wasn't Mickey?" she asked.

"We just do." Greg patted her shoulder.

George walked over and kicked Mickey's leg. "You could look at it this way. You got him back for Shirley."

There was that, but now there was someone else out there she had to find.

And she would. However long it took.

# Chapter Fifty-Six

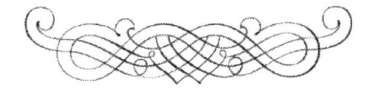

In Jonathan's house, Rebecca clasped her hands in her lap. She sat in the old battered armchair by the fire as if it were the most natural thing in the world. "I would've thought you'd have been to our house long before now, but I'm wondering if you love Gracie like you say you do. After her guessing you were married, and you not coming round to make the peace, she and I were…well, I don't know what we were thinking."

"I was going to come and see you today to explain," he said. "I didn't intend for her to find out, but I didn't have the heart to lie anymore."

"You could have told a little white lie, just to save her getting hurt. She's in a right mess," Rebecca said. "She's keeping the baby, but as for seeing you, I think you'd have to go a long way to make her forgive you. You don't know how hard it's been for me not to jump to your defence in telling her that Leona is an old bag you hate, and you only married her because of the circumstances. As I told you, I've kept my mouth well and truly shut on the subject of knowing about your marriage. I won't become involved in that. I'll lose my daughter's trust, if not lose her altogether."

"Do you think she'll see me, to let me at least try to explain?"

"Look, what I'll do is see how the land lies. I'll tell her I bumped into you today, and you explained all about your marriage. What *is* going to happen, though, Jonathan?"

This was at least something he could say which might tip the scales in his favour. "I've been and arranged an annulment. She's signed it, but it might be a while."

A look of horror passed over her face. "A *while*?"

"Hmm." He changed the subject. "It's funny, but since I moved back here, I've found out more about Leona than I did when I lived there. She's been left all the pubs but one, and a little bird told me she's selling them, bar The Eagle."

"She's selling?"

She gave him a weird smile, but he didn't question it. There were more important things to do. Like getting back with Gracie.

# Chapter Fifty-Seven

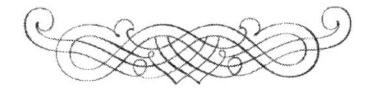

The letterbox clattered, and Leona winced at the sound of the post plopping on the mat. Out in the hallway, she scooped the letters up and went back to her seat in the living room. There it was, the cream envelope, peeping out at her from between the other smaller ones. Did she really need to read it? Contemplating putting it into the fire, she changed her mind. Curiosity got the better of her. She took out the bumpy note. Lots of glue again.

NON-CONSUMMATION? IT DOESN'T SURPRISE ME.
WHO'D WANT TO TOUCH YOU?

That hurt. It really hurt.

She threw the paper into the fire, determined not to be upset by the malicious notes any longer. She pressed on with sorting out the other letters. By the time she'd read the last one, she'd had enough. Life was really throwing its worst at her.

It was from a solicitor, informing her that dear, dense Sam was dead.

---

After months of being apart from Gracie and putting off collecting the last of his belongings from the marital home, Jonathan bit the bullet and returned.

"How about taking me to a Christmas ball," Leona asked. "For old time's sake. The least we could do is become friends."

What was up with *her*, suggesting that? "I've only dropped in to pick up some of my things. And no, I won't take you."

"Am I allowed to know why not?"

Irritation surged inside him. "Because I've left you and don't want to be seen out with you in public. Good enough reason for you?"

"Oh, well. I did try to do it nicely." She walked off into the kitchen, smirking.

*God, I fucking hate her.*

"I've had a bid for the pubs," she called through, "from an anonymous buyer. It's a good price, so I think I might sell. Maybe after the annulment, though."

"I don't want any of your money, if that's what you're thinking. Go ahead and sell now. I couldn't care less."

"I can't guarantee they'll still buy your beer."

"You've only been buying my beer to keep my mouth shut anyway," he shouted.

"You know me well."

He went upstairs and gathered his things, then made his way to the kitchen. "Right, I've got my stuff, so I'm off."

"Are you sure you won't change your mind about taking me to the ball? It's for a good cause. You aren't going with anyone else by any chance?"

"I don't even know what bloody ball you're on about, so if you don't mind, I'm going. I'll see myself out."

---

Gracie stared at the table, downcast.

"I did tell him I'd told you everything, love. I'm sure he'll come and see you one day soon," Mum said.

"But how long is he going to leave it? I've sent him texts and everything, letting him know we need to talk. The baby will be born before he turns up."

"All I know is that he said soon."

The doorbell rang its jolly jingle. God, the last thing Gracie needed was to make small talk with one of her mother's friends.

Mum got up to answer the door, coming back into the living room, a smug grin in place. "I said it would be soon, but I didn't realise how soon."

Gracie looked up and knew when she saw Jonathan standing there she could forgive him.

Mum left the room.

He explained. Gracie forgave.

Rebecca was busy in her study. Gracie and Jonathan would be in the lounge for a while to come. She was safe to do her little note.

"It's all coming to an end, Leona," she said quietly. "Soon, I'll have got you back. And serves you right."

Finished, she waved the paper in front of the fire. Happy the glue had dried, she addressed the envelope and popped the note inside. It had given her a fit of the giggles this time. Surely Leona would guess who'd been sending them now.

Time would tell.

"I'm just going out to the postbox," she called, smiling when she got no answer.

Gracie and Jonathan were busy, sorting out the rest of their lives.

While Rebecca was busy sorting out hers.

UGLY LITTLE LEONA, HANGING ROUND AT SCHOOL
PROFESSING LOVE TO OTHERS, SHE IS SUCH A FOOL
ENDING UP WITH NO ONE, THROUGH LONELINESS SHE'LL WADE

## UGLY HORSEY LEONA, THE HAGGY OLD MAID

"Nothing better to do with their time," Leona said.

The flames were consuming the note as reality dawned.

It was that damn Rebecca sending the notes.

Dashing forward, she tried to get the half-burnt paper out of the fire, but the tongs wouldn't grip it. She'd go to the police. Tell them all about the woman who'd been hounding her for months with poison pen letters.

Reality dawned again. She couldn't do it. She had no evidence.

She had burnt each and every one.

# Chapter Fifty-Eight

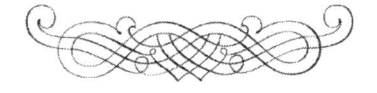

Harry still couldn't get over Mickey running off like that. The stupid bastard must have got cold feet because of the rumours going round that he'd killed Cardigan. Harry hadn't even offered to put the record straight now that Sam was dead—he was the only one to fear reprisals from. The Brothers were in on it and wouldn't give him any hassle.

He reckoned he ought to feel guilty but didn't. The thing was, Mickey had his own mind, and if he'd decided to fuck off into the sunset and start a new life elsewhere, good luck to him. Harry missed him, though, had been at a loose end to begin with, but Greg and George had taken him under their wing, giving him a job now they'd taken over the manor.

Harry wasn't stupid. He knew it was to keep him close. Let him know they were breathing down his neck despite them being happy he'd offed Cardigan.

It'd be all right. He'd keep his mouth shut, act dumb when people asked him if he knew who'd done it if it wasn't Mickey. That Debbie bird, Peony, she'd come along to his gaff with her questions, but he'd put on an act and made out he was clueless.

He had a feeling she might cause him some problems if she kept digging, but he'd deal with her if it came to that. Shame, because she was an all right sort really, and he wouldn't mind having her all to himself in the parlour.

Maybe that was what he'd do. Wheedle his way in, keep her sweet, at the same time finding out her plans on how she'd catch Cardigan's killer.

If The Brothers had taught him one thing, it was to keep your enemies close.

Well, give him time, and he'd be as close to Debbie as he could get.

# Chapter Fifty-Nine

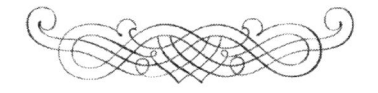

December already.

Rebecca and Gracie stood in the entrance of the ballroom at The Grafton, ready to greet the guests. A Christmas tree stood in the corner, festooned with large red-and-gold balls, thick tinsel, and hundreds of fairy lights. A huge balloon net filled to the brim hung down, ready for later when everyone was in high spirits.

Many donated gifts sat on the auction table, waiting for the wealthy to bid for them. Rebecca was planning to have a brand-new building built for the homeless.

She automatically went into host mode, smiling until her face stiffened, shaking hands until her arms ached.

A breeze of men and women entered, and by half seven, Gracie looked apprehensive.

"What time did Jonathan say he was coming?" Rebecca asked.

"He didn't…"

"Mr Rogers, how wonderful." Rebecca smiled at the man in front of her, gritting her teeth. If Jonathan let her daughter down again, she'd swing for him. Grin permanently fixed, she greeted on.

Then he came through the doors, rushing in with that incorrigible smile of his.

*It's all right, it's going to be fine.*

Rebecca glanced over at Gracie. "What is it, darling? Is it the baby?"

Looking back at Jonathan, Rebecca found her answer.

She'd be swinging for him all right.

Jonathan walked closer to Rebecca and Gracie. "What?" he said, laughing. "What are you looking at me like that for?"

"Jonathan," Leona said, "don't walk off. You're always leaving me behind."

*Leona?*

He turned. "What the hell d'you think you're playing at turning up here?"

She smiled. "Whatever do you mean? You asked me to come."

He spun to Gracie, fucking fuming. "You've got to believe me. I didn't know she was coming."

Gracie and Leona glared at him with hate.

"Really, Jonathan. You should have known better," Rebecca said.

Pale, Gracie barged past Leona. Jonathan followed, leaving Rebecca and Leona facing one another. Gracie dashed into a taxi, and it pulled off. Another came along, but Leona rushed out of The Grafton and got in.

She wound down the window. "Upset, are we, darling?"

Jonathan wanted to kill her. "Piss off, you nasty bitch."

"Drive on, cabbie," she said and closed the window.

He stood there, at a loss. What the fuck was he meant to do now?

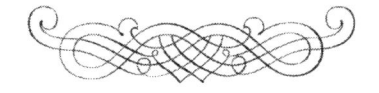

# Chapter Sixty

February had arrived so quickly. The tiny girl was beautiful, and Gracie couldn't believe it was all over.

"Well done, darling. I'm so proud of you," Mum said.

Gracie gazed down at her new baby. She was the image of her father, downy hair in soft tufts.

Even squashed up and with her head out of shape, she was a wonder.

Gracie's emotions when she'd left The Grafton that night were indescribable. The tears didn't come straight away. She was so shocked she found it hard to determine just what she'd been feeling. Hate, certainly. An all-consuming hate for Jonathan and his lies. Telling her they'd start from scratch, when all along he'd been playing games, bringing his wife with him.

*Just what he'd hoped to gain she didn't know, and as the taxi pulled up outside her home, she got out, paid, and went indoors, the chill of the evening clutching at her like witches' fingers. She stood looking at herself in the hallway mirror, startled, eyes wide.*

*Lifting her dress, she studied her bump. She had no man to help raise her baby. And thank goodness for that. She didn't want to tell her child that its father had been a bastard, using her and lying through his teeth.*

*She walked up the stairs, and the tears came then, sudden and without warning. For all he had shown himself to be, God help her, she still loved him. She was sure he* was *a wonderful and caring man, but his behaviour that evening had proved otherwise. And she'd have to live with it.*

*He tried to ring her many times, sending texts. Her answer was always the same. Go away. Even when he'd told Mum he was now free from Leona, after a slight glimmer of hope, Gracie had told her to say she wasn't interested. She couldn't trust him again. She'd done that once already, and look where that had got her. Nowhere but hurt and broken.*

She was so beautiful, this baby girl. Should she deny her the father who was hers by right? Or should she let them form some kind of bond so Gracie wasn't reproached in years to come?

Yes, she'd have to let father and daughter meet.

"Ring Jonathan at his office, Mum. He needs to know she's here."

---

Rebecca would never forgive Leona for as long as she lived. Turning up at the ball like that, destroying her daughter's life. How dare she?

She'd long since believed Jonathan when he'd pleaded over the phone that it had all been a big mistake. He hadn't known Leona was coming. Everything had been finalised, and he was free to be with Gracie.

He wouldn't give up, she'd give him that. He was intent on making Gracie his wife. He had it all planned, he'd said. And Rebecca knew if he'd just give her daughter time, one day she'd listen.

Rebecca wasn't about to let Leona win.

The envelope she'd been given by Leona before she'd marched out, triumphant from The Grafton, had nearly boiled her blood. Leona thought she was so clever, but Rebecca had wanted her to know it'd been her who'd sent the notes. And Leona knew all right.

Opening the envelope, Rebecca had looked inside a card with a queen chess piece on the front. In carefully cut-out newspaper letters, it read: CHECKMATE.

"I'll give you checkmate," she'd seethed. "I won when I bought your pubs, you stupid bloody woman."

She picked up the phone to dial Jonathan's number.

---

As Jonathan was about to lock the office, the desk phone rang. He turned back and picked up the receiver. "Hello?"

"Hello." Rebecca. "You have a daughter."

His stomach flipped over. "How…how is Gracie?"

"She wants to see you. Let you meet the baby."

Relief. A breakthrough. "When?"

"Now?"

"I'll be there in five minutes."

Hands shaking, heart pumping, he got into his car and sped off in the direction of the Lynchwood's. He'd make Gracie see everything could be all right. He had so much to say to her, he didn't know where to begin. But Rebecca had said she wanted him to meet the baby. Was that all it was?

*But it's a start.*

Pulling up outside the house, he took a deep breath and walked up to the front door. He went to knock, but a midwife came bustling out, tired-looking but with a smile.

"Are you the father?" she asked, all jovial.

"I am."

"Well, you'd better get on in. They're waiting for you so they can name her. She's a little Miss Nobody at the moment."

He stepped inside and closed the front door, spotting Rebecca in the kitchen, putting the kettle on, and she turned, pointing upwards. Grateful she was using tact in allowing him to go up alone, he smiled at her and ascended the stairs.

He approached Gracie's room. Small sniffles came from inside. Alarmed she might be crying, he pushed the door open just a little, relieved it wasn't her. She was fast asleep in a sitting position against the pillows.

The baby snuffled, eyes closed, rubbing her little fists on her mouth. His baby. His girl. He walked over to the Moses basket beside the bed and gazed down. Immediately, love hit him. He wouldn't be able to live a life seeing her only sometimes. On weekends. He wanted to watch this prized bundle grow up. Wanted her to know her daddy—as a daddy not a stranger she was shy with at first until she got used to him again.

He rubbed his palms together to get them warm. He was going to pick his girl up, give her the first of many cuddles. Shower her with all the love. Give her the love he couldn't give her mother, because she wouldn't let him.

He reached down and placed his hands around his child and brought her to his chest. Gingerly, he moved her so she was comfortable, afraid to break her. Afraid to hurt her. She was so fucking precious. He'd do anything to protect her. Lay down his life.

He sat on the bed and stared down on her again. Button nose, dinky ears, dainty fingers. Oh, she was lovely, beautiful. The best baby in the world. Because she was his. His and Gracie's, and they'd made her together.

"Isn't she lovely?"

Jonathan jumped, startled that Gracie was awake. How long had she been watching him?

*She* was beautiful, too. A new mother. His heart contracted with so much love for his two girls he reckoned it'd burst. He had to make her see it.

"Just like her mother," he said quietly.

"I'm sorry, Jonathan…"

Panicked, he said, "I know things went wrong, but I want to work it out."

"What shall we call her?"

It only took a moment for him to think of a name. One that summed up everything he felt. "Hope."

"Hope it is then."

"Will we…?"

Gracie shook her head, and despite his joy at having his daughter in his arms, Jonathan's world crumbled.

---

All right, Rebecca wasn't going to do this, but one more little dig with the knife wouldn't hurt, would it?

Placing the folded white paper in the envelope, she went out to the postbox.

---

Leona opened the envelope and pulled out the card. She'd put the past behind her, and now it all came tumbling back. Rebecca was up to her old tricks, restarting the war between them. Tears sprang to her eyes as she read the card. Would she ever be happy in her life? Would she ever know the joy these people were feeling now? And it was *Gracie* all along? God…

JONATHAN AND GRACIE PROUDLY
ANNOUNCE
THE BIRTH OF THEIR DAUGHTER, HOPE

# Chapter Sixty-One

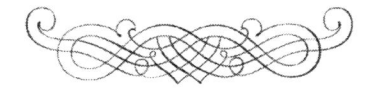

Debbie sat at the bar in The Angel an hour before the shift started in the parlour. The place was packed. She'd taken to having discos on Friday, Saturday, and Sunday nights, and with the pub being just along the way from the nightclub, people squeezed inside to get pissed-up, giving their body the fuel to keep them warm while standing in the long queue outside. The weather was shocking, so cold she shivered at night even with the heating on fifteen and a great big duvet over her.

Harry had been trying to get cosy with her a month or so after Mickey went 'missing', and she'd rebuffed him so far, saying she didn't want another emotional attachment so soon after Cardigan's death. But last night—or the early hours when she'd stared at the ceiling waiting for sleep to come—she'd thought of something. From the shifty way Harry acted every time she'd mentioned Mickey killing Cardigan, she was sure he knew something.

What if she let him into her life, making out they were a couple, playing out the whole charade with him thinking she trusted him enough that he'd admit who'd done it?

Hence her sitting here now. Harry was due any minute, and she glanced at the massive clock to count down the seconds. With two to go, she looked in the mirror behind the bar and watched the double doors as best she could, what with people standing in front of them. Harry was tall, and she spotted the top of his head when he arrived. He pushed through the crowd and stood beside her, smiling.

"What's all this about?" he asked.

*Wouldn't you like to know.* She smiled back and settled her arm in the crook of his. "I've had another think about your offer. You know, us getting together."

His eyebrows rose. "Really?"

"Hmm. I'm willing if you are." She stroked his arm.

He grinned so wide she almost felt sorry for him. This would be so easy.

"Too fucking right I am," he said.

She sealed it with a kiss, all the while thinking: *Let the game begin.*

Printed in Great Britain
by Amazon